CITY ANOINTED

CITY ANOINTED

SPIRITUAL WARFARE FOR A CITY

a novel by

MICHAEL BURROWS

A CHRISTIAN FANTASY/REALITY NOVEL

 MIKE BURROWS GRAPHICS

First Printing: November 2022

ISBN 978-0-473-65706-2 (Paperback)
ISBN 978-0-473-65707-9 (Epub)

www.afreshstartbook.com
info@afreshstartbook.com

*This book is dedicated to
my wife and three children, and to all those
who fearlessly engage in the spiritual battle
through faith, prayer and love.*

CONTENTS

1

MOUNTAINSIDE

Liberty leapt off the path and skidded down the steep embankment. The gravel ground beneath her boots as she slid. She dropped off the ledge and landed on the uneven rock below.

Scree lay in drifts down the ancient mountainside, making the ground unstable. But Liberty was a seasoned warrior, she could handle herself through this terrain. Having already traversed the spirit world to save one city, Liberty had the experience to take on this mission and save another.

Her lonely figure cast a long shadow across the landscape, as she hurried through the maze of broken rock, outpacing and outmanoeuvring her pursuers. She ran up a slab of rock then launched into an aerial cartwheel off the edge. Landing in a crouched position, with fingertips splayed out to steady herself, she took a breather for a moment. Liberty puffed the hair away from her face, then remaining very still, she closed her eyes and listened for the enemy. Faint footsteps indicated that she was maintaining a good distance between herself and them. She pounced back into action and continued her descent.

Liberty quickly ran into a ravine carved into the mountainside. With arms stretched out to steady herself, she slipped around boulders and over slabs of heavy grey slate. In front of her, a pile of loose rocks were heaped up at one end. Liberty stepped onto the pile of rock and slapped her hands against slate walls. Then pushing up with all of her might, she launched herself through the gap.

The ground below was a lot further away than she had anticipated. Liberty gasped, landing on her feet momentarily, she lost her footing and fell onto her side with a thud. The loose gravel swept her toward the edge of the cliff which fell away far below. Her body scraped down the steep bank, sending her hurtling down the mountainside. With only moments before falling off the edge and into the endless expanse, she had the presence of mind to draw a knife that was strapped to her thigh, roll over, and drive it into the ground. Immediately she slowed and came to a halt as her legs rolled over the edge of the cliff, dangling above deep darkness. She hoisted herself back over the ledge and looked up. Three figures were fast approaching.

Liberty was now trapped between the outer boundary of the realm, and the three attackers in front. With nowhere to go, Liberty prepared to engage.

She whispered a prayer, "A little help would be nice right now!"

***

Back on-surface, Aria was rushing to get to work early. A bus splashed through a puddle and delivered a black cloud of exhaust fumes in front of her as she stepped out onto the road. As Aria skipped up the footpath on the other side, Liberty's face flashed across her mind. 'Wonder what you are doing today Lib?' she thought.

Aria entered the deserted shopping complex. She was often the first to open up shop. She turned the key in the lock at the bottom of the roller doors, and began lifting it. The metal grating rose up and recoiled around the top roller. Once it was fully retracted, she stepped forward, pushing through the double doors in the glass frontage and strode into the store. Again, Liberty's name came to her mind.

Aria prayed out loud, "Lord, I pray that you would bless, help, and protect Liberty today."

A flicker of light sparked around Aria like an electrical charge. Her prayer sprung to life. The charge conducted along the metal clothes hangers as she breezed past.

"I like you," she said pointing to a denim jacket hanging against the wall – a new season arrival. As she walked through the store, she felt the urge to continue praying, so took out a minute or two to do just that. Aria started to pace and pray for her friend at the back of the store.

"Lord, fill Liberty with your grace and with faith to achieve all that you want her to achieve today. Fill her again with your Spirit, and empower her to be victorious to accomplish your purposes…"

Her prayer-form, the visual substance of her prayer, ignited her surroundings with electrical pulses that sent shockwaves out in all directions. The power of her prayer couldn't be seen by the natural eye, but veins of light flashed, plainly obvious to the spirit realm. Electricity from her prayer-form arced in an array of light all around. Charges danced through her fingers and flickered through her hair. Then something else started to happen. As she reached a deeper level of prayer and intercession, and all this within a minute or two, six shapes arose from the ground around her – lions. The lions faced outwards, and rose within the midst of the electrical storm. The fur on the creatures bristled with energy and the lion's manes, layered with light, were tossed about in the storm.

As Aria felt the leading of the Holy Spirit, she commanded the situation to conform to the purposes of God, and clapped her hands together once. As she clapped, the build-up of energy in the room was released. The lions roared and leapt into the air. Electricity continued to arc around them and splay outwards conducting through the atmosphere, causing the fluorescent tubes in the room to light up and the light bulbs to flicker. A final charge of energy exploded, and the lions were launched into the dawn.

"Amen. Done!" stated Aria. "Well, that was exciting," she said, feeling like something had happened. Even though she had no idea of the actual power that she possessed through her unique prayer-form, she felt that her prayer had been noticed by God.

'Hope Lib is okay. I'll message her and find out how she is,' she thought. 'Next… t-shirts.' Aria lifted out a stack of new t-shirts from a box in the storeroom that had been delivered the day before, and brought them into the shop.

***

Liberty rose to her feet, and planted her boots on a slab of slate. Suddenly electricity exploded around her; the empowering prayer of her friend.

Liberty lowered her eyebrows. A phrase from the Bible pierced her mind like a sword being driven into her thoughts from heaven's throne, 'See, the Lion of the tribe of Judah, the Root of David, has triumphed.' Liberty sheathed her knife with one hand, and unsheathed her sword with the other. She exhaled as she rushed forward. Her breath unexpectedly rolled into a growl. Liberty skipped from rock to rock. Her eyelids narrowed, tightly framing her eyes. Her glassy eyes turned a wild yellow colour, brighter toward the centre like a dazzling star. They flashed with faith. The Spirit of the Lion of the Tribe of Judah rose from within her. The lion's legs were her legs, the lion's muscles were her muscles, and the lion's heart was her heart. The glow of glory around her was like a lion's mane, full of light.

As her pursuers crested the hill, their expressions completely changed from evil savagery into absolute fear. All three stumbled over each other in shock. They slid down the bank toward her, desperately clawing at the loose ground in an attempt to get away. Too late for the first. Liberty swung her blade and slashed through the first demon's mid-section, releasing a crackling of electrical sparks. The two halves continued to slide past her and drop off the precipice. The other two managed to stop and stumble up to their feet. The demon to her left raised its jagged blade, but Liberty struck first and knocked the sword from its hand, releasing a flash of lightning. Then in one motion she spun around, drawing her blade through the bony body to finish it off. The third demon fell backwards, regained composure, and managed to scuttle a safe distance away from the girl.

The demon then reached out its arms as if ready to receive something. Suddenly from nowhere shadows flew into it from all directions. Shadowy bats appeared as blurs and rushed toward the creature, becoming a part of it, and causing it to grow.

Now twice the size, the demon stood in front of her, looking down and despising this young girl.

Then it spoke with a deep voice, "Your foundations are just dust!"

Liberty stared back with a golden fiery gaze, her eyes blazing with the glory of God. Golden sparks emanated from the centre of her eyes, splaying outwards like shooting stars streaking across her iris.

"I am made in the image of my creator. My foundations are in Him," she declared.

"You failed!" it shouted.

"I know," responded Liberty.

"If He charges His angels with error, how much more you!" it said.

"You still sore about that?" replied Liberty. "Your error in joining darkness, and losing your place in heaven and all?"

"Careful girl. You're talking about things you know nothing of."

"From streets of gold to muddy boots. How does it taste? The mud I mean."

"Your flesh is from the mud!"

"At least I can be forgiven. That's one thing I do know."

"He will never forgive you. You let down an entire city. It's in our hands now," it retorted. "You've changed the course of history. The city is ours and it will be laid to ashes."

"Jesus covers it!" Liberty shot back, fighting back the heavy, condemning emotions that were trying to find a place within her soul. Her confidence was slipping a little, but the words from her mouth flowed out from what was deep in her spirit.

"No he won't! He won't cover it. You're a failure, a sinner. You lost!" The demon spat as it shouted.

That was a mistake, calling Liberty a sinner. She understood her identity, and knew that God no longer saw her as a sinner.

"No, I am not! I have a new identity. I'm not a sinner, I'm a new creation. I read my Bible."

"I know that book better than you," it said.

"Perhaps. But you only know the words. You have no revelation from it," Liberty responded.

"It doesn't change the fact that you lost, you failed."

Then in a moment of unfolding revelation, and being carried along by the Spirit, Liberty said, "You mean like those others who failed, Moses, David, Peter? Those whom God attributed friendship, people after his own heart, those on whom he will build his church?

"You are deluded," it shouted back. "You are nothing compared to them."

Liberty knew she was being caught in a loop of accusations, and she needed to pull herself free. In righteous anger, Liberty responded, "I do not compare myself to the heroes of faith. I know who I am. I am redeemed, I am sanctified, I am a child of God, I hold his attention, nothing can separate me from his love, his purposes, his calling. Get behind me Satan. I am marked with the seal of the Holy Spirit within me, guaranteeing my eternal inheritance with the saints. I am chosen, set apart, and called to this mission, and with the help of God I shall achieve victory for the glory of my God! Now go, in Jesus name!"

With that, the ground started to shake and threw Liberty off her feet. As Liberty looked up, she saw how powerful her words were. The demon stood with legs apart, trying to keep its balance. Then it looked at her in shock as all colour fled from its body, like a cloth being snatched from a table. Its soul was wrenched from what had been its habitation, and the demon in front of her turned into stone. Bits of it exploded into fragments. A shoulder burst and its heavy arm dropped to the ground. Then its side blew out into tiny fragments. The demon's neck shattered, causing the head to be flung backwards. Then the rest of it collapsed into pieces and scattered on the ground.

Liberty was full of adrenaline having uttered words that she never thought she could against her accuser. Everything around her was still shaking, but her heart felt secure knowing that she had just overcome the enemy by the word of her mouth and the authority Jesus had given her. Liberty stood to her feet as the rumbling settled.

The storm of faith within Liberty gently subsided. Her hair swayed in the breeze as the winds eased.

After some time of standing on the mountainside alone, she tilted her head heavenward, "Have I really failed God?"

Silence.

Liberty suddenly felt quite alone and defeated. One moment she felt full of the power of God, and the next moment all her strength seemed to be sapped away. The feeling of being a complete failure settled over her like a heavy blanket. Now, it was like all the past victories were long forgotten. Even though she had achieved so much, in this moment, she felt like it had all been useless.

The assignment set for Liberty was to find the keys. She had been so close. She knew where they were, or at least had been. If the demons already had them, then she had failed her mission. 'Is it possible to steal them back?' she thought. 'But there's no time, the demons will take them straight to the altar and use them against the city.'

"Now what do I do?" she said, turning her face to the night sky. The stars that sparkled in the vast emptiness didn't answer her.

"Is there any hope?"

Then, on a distant breeze, she heard far-off voices being carried on the winds. In the midst of the emptiness around her, she closed her eyes and strained her ears to hear the dark whispers echo.

"The city falls today," she heard. "The great annihilation has begun." Then she caught faint shouts and roars which trailed off into the distance, reverberating out of the realm.

2

GENEVA

"**N**early home girl," John said, reassuring his horse. He grabbed hold of the horse's wet bridle, and pulled the horse up the narrow winding track toward Geneva. John was tired, having walked most of the way. "I'll see to that hoof of yours when we get back," he said, looking down at the horse's front right front hoof which was causing irritation.

'Nearly home' is of course relative, depending on how far the entire journey has been. If he had been on a short journey, then 'nearly home' would only be a short distance, perhaps ten or fifteen minutes, as was the case today. But in recent years John had been on much longer journeys. He had travelled across France, from Paris to Strasbourg, and then was forced to make a detour into Switzerland. His travels weren't exactly going according to plan, but John did love to see the Gentian flowers of the Swiss countryside. Bright blue pops of colour were scattered over the grass, and the flowers that lined the edges of the path quivered in the breeze.

John exhaled a misty puff of air as he walked, and turned to watch it evaporate into the morning behind. The tip of his nose felt frozen and he sneezed, then sniffed, while the wind flapped his jacket.

John's clothes were dampening by the minute, so he picked up the pace, not wanting to end up soaking wet by the time he got back to his house. His buttoned waistcoat was defence against the chilly breeze, but it also felt uncomfortable, as he was sweating at the same time. The white shirt underneath his waistcoat was of course no longer white. It had been his travel companion on many such journeys. It kept a visual diary of past falls and scrapes, and now was also heavily infused with sweat.

Leading his horse under a low hanging branch, John raised his hand to brush it out of the way. As the damp leaves slapped his shoulder, a sudden chill raced down his spine. His heart jumped and his eyes widened as he snapped his head around to look in all directions.

"Who's there!" he called out. He stood still as his horse stomped and snorted. "Shhh," he scolded. Motionless, apart from his eyes scanning over the trees, he looked and listened. All was quiet. Suddenly he thought he heard a whisper in the breeze, the echo of some distant voice being carried on the winds. The voice didn't belong, it was an intrusion in his land. A wandering whisper that had yet to settle, looking for a place or a person to torment. An invader from the far off shadow realms. John's eyes flicked from the path, to the nearby trees scattered amongst grass and bushes. He couldn't see very far into the woods. 'Too many blind spots,' he thought.

John was wary of raiders and thieves that would come to these parts, waiting for farmers or traders to pass by. The thieves would take anything of value from travellers, including food and supplies. Even basic food was scarce at times, so it was always wise for a traveller to hide a little extra in a saddle bag or at the bottom of a sack. Having various places to store food meant that a thief might only find some of the supplies, while other provisions would be kept safe, secretly hidden away.

John was feeling very uneasy. 'Am I in danger?' he thought. He was aware of a presence, but it didn't feel like raiders, it felt more like a dark mist reaching out icy fingers toward him.

Only a few feet away from where he was standing, a menacing creature was lurking in the shadow of a tree, just to the side of the path. Its lanky dark blue form was taller than John. It had long thin claws protruding from its fingers, with similar looking talons arching off the back of its head like pointed dreadlocks. Its face was cone-shaped and had a long pointed nose and chin, with a slanted back forehead. Its yellow breath leached out between its teeth as it looked at John in disgust.

The demon wasn't in the slightest trying to conceal itself, because it couldn't be seen by humans. This creature required a high level of discernment to detect it. John was unaware of the fact that a demonic beast stood just a few feet away from him. Yet, he could feel its evil presence and it caused him to shiver.

John remained motionless. Intimidation slowly turned into determination as he gritted his teeth. Seeing nothing, and hearing no other movements, he quickly stepped forward and continued hastily through the wooded area toward the outskirts of town.

'A very strange encounter,' thought John. 'Strange indeed.' He glanced back the way he had come. The path wound through quiet trees. There was no other noise, apart from the gentle cold breeze rustling the leaves.

"You never know what you're going to find in these woods," said John to his horse, trying to comfort himself, just as much as his four-legged friend. "I just need to get home to a warm fire," he said, as he emerged from the tree-line and continued to lead his horse toward home.

"Not long now," John said, patting the horse's neck. "Not long now."

Out of natural sight, the tall, slender shadow remained for a while. As John trudged off into the distance, the creature turned away and walked back into the woods. As it did, the demon passed through beams of dawn that shone between leaves and branches. The diagonal beams fell across the figure, making it translucent in the light, but solid in the shadow. As it passed through patches of light and shadow, the creature faded in and out, almost disappearing in the sunlight, and reappearing in the shade. Tossed between two worlds, it paced through the trees.

Then finding deep-shadow, just before fading out of earth-realm, it whispered, "We're about to take you out John. Out for good."

***

John arrived home, hung up his coat, and filled a jug with water. He carried the jug over to the open fireplace and set it on the iron grill that was fixed above the burning embers. He placed a couple of pieces of wood onto the coals, and settled into his armchair. Within a couple of minutes the flames burst into life, and within a few more minutes the boiling water was ready to pour.

Sipping on his cup of tea, he pondered the meeting he had just had with his friend William. William had such a passion for the gospel and was working hard to build the church in the city in which they lived.

William had convinced John to partner with him in advancing the work of the kingdom of God in the city. John had not planned on staying in the area at all. After returning from overseas the year before, he had intended to make only a fleeting visit. He was on his way to some remote location, away from the eyes of the world, to apply himself to his passion for study. John loved to study the scriptures and write his own commentaries on the Bible.

Nevertheless, William had convinced John to stay, and even called it 'his Christian duty', to help influence the city and contend for the gospel. At this time, there was a great openness to the message of Christianity, and William's church was full week after week, with people accepting the good news of the gospel.

William and John were both respected, and loathed, by members of the City Council. There was adversity to the gospel among some. But within the majority of the council, there was a willingness to accept the modern teachings of William and John. Unfortunately those who were against the gospel tended to be the loudest and often swayed public opinion.

Yet it had all come down to this. In just two days, was the meeting of the City Council of Geneva, where both John and William would present their documents to them all. Should these documents be accepted, the city would embrace the reformed theology of John and William, and officially become a centre of religious activity for the entire country.

John and William's confession of faith included the fact that

Christians are saved by grace alone through faith, not by good works. The good works which flow out of a Christian life are simply an expression of the transformation within. But the good works themselves are not a requirement for salvation. The document also stated that the Bible is the highest authority. It is the divine unchanging Word of God.

John also drafted a supplementary document about the organisation of the church, including how to run church services, and how praise and worship should be conducted.

If these documents were to be accepted, it would change much of the societal structure of the city. It could possibly influence the entire country, and perhaps even change the course of history for the entire known world.

John took another sip of tea and placed his cup on the small wooden table beside him. He leaned his head back in the armchair and closed his eyes.

***

Two tormenting demons looked through the window at John resting in his armchair. They were about to claw their way into the house when they noticed John's lips starting to move.

"No! He's not going to start praying is he?" said one to the other.

"Argh - he is!" said the other demon in alarm. "We're going to be punished for this if we can't get in there and take away his peace." The demons lost no time in quickly pushing their way into the house to reach John before he started to pray. Scrambling toward the armchair, they raised their claws in an attempt to plunge in doubt and discharge fear... but too late...

John prayed, "Lord, may the council meeting be favourable, for the sake of this city, for the sake of your city. You've called me here to make a difference, and make a difference we must..."

His prayer-form began to shift the spiritual mechanics of the atmosphere around him. The demons who had got so close, were now being edged back by John's expanding prayer-form. They looked at each other defeated because they knew they had just lost the game. There was no way that they would be able to get close to him now.

John's prayer grew and expanded around him like a giant compass with interlocking wheels. The demons were forced backwards by the energy in John's prayer. One demon got caught between two rotating cogs and was crushed as they rolled against each other. A faint cry and puff of smoke rose from the crumpled figure as it disintegrated into dust and gas. The other demon escaped the dangerous mechanics of John's prayer-form, but was pushed outside the house, far out of any ability to influence John's thinking and emotions.

The outermost expanding circle had compass points indicating the four natural directions of North, South, West and East. The inner wheels indicated other spiritual directions that marked out significant points across the spiritual landscape. Within these wheels, a clock face also expanded around him. His 'prayer-form', initiated great changes in times and seasons.

While the compass wheels rose and expanded around him, arcs swept over his head like enormous revolving gyroscopes. His prayer continued to grow to surround his whole house, then reached out across streets, over fields, and across the lake, until it almost encircled the entire city. The curved golden gyroscopic beams rose and fell over the buildings, reflecting the light as they moved along their course, casting reflections and shadows across the city.

***

From another vantage point, Liberty and her friends were looking out over Geneva, getting an understanding of what their mission would be.

John's prayer held long enough for them to see the spiritual layout of the city. They could see the points of the compass, and the significant spiritual landmarks that would be the focal points of their separate missions. The clock indicated two days until a shift, either for good or for evil. They were thankful for John's prayer displaying the paths that each of them should take. They tried to take everything in, committing to memory where they needed to go.

3

ANNIVERSARY

The year had gone quickly since the epic crusade that Liberty's friend Layla had powerfully spoken at. With Layla's dad having his flight delayed, Layla had bravely stepped in, and presented an amazing and well received gospel message. Since then, so much had happened and Liberty barely had time to do anything else apart from studying hard for her degree in physiotherapy, and being involved in all the activity of church. The youth group had doubled in size since this time last year with a whole bunch of new Christians. Liberty was also leading a couple of discipleship courses, and looking after some new Life Groups which had sprung up in various places within her community.

Liberty was excited because today was the day. Today she was going to get together with her friends Layla, Trinity, Samantha, Tristan and Caden to commemorate their adventure a year earlier, when they had saved Riverdale. It seemed like a lifetime ago, but Liberty's relationship with the Holy Spirit had continued to deepen since that time. Angel light still flicked past her every now and then, but she hadn't seen Falcon since their adventure.

From time to time she would wonder to herself, 'What are you doing right now Falcon? Are you fighting epic battles, destroying demons, and extending the kingdom of God across many realms? Or are you in the presence of God, in his throne room, enveloped in the brightest light deep in the centre of heaven?'

Liberty shrugged, 'Maybe you are sitting on the banks of the River of Life. Just chillin'. Can't be action all the time like a celestial social media highlight reel. I'm sure you also have those regular heaven days, where endless colours roll over the ethereal skies, and scented winds breathe fresh life into the inhabitants. Yep, just normal heaven days,' she thought with a sigh and a smile.

Every so often she felt urged to pray for Falcon, wherever he might be, that he would be aided in his quests. Liberty often recalled verses from the book of Daniel:

> *So he said, "Do you know why I have come to you? Soon I will return*
> *to fight against the prince of Persia, and when I go, the prince of*
> *Greece will come; but first I will tell you what is written in the Book*
> *of Truth. (No one supports me against them except Michael, your*
> *prince. And in the first year of Darius the Mede, I took my stand to*
> *support and protect him.)*

Liberty felt that the Holy Spirit had highlighted to her that last sentence, and she decided to take her stand to support Falcon and other angels through prayer, to aid them in their quests.

***

Her friends were due to arrive in a couple of hours. Liberty took a pizza from a shelf in the freezer and popped it in the oven. She headed down the hallway for a shower, scooping up a pair of her brother's shorts that were lying on the floor with her foot, flicking them into her hand, and throwing them into the washing basket as she passed the laundry.

She had the house to herself for the weekend because her parents and brother had gone to stay with her grandparents out of town. It was her brother's birthday yesterday and her grandparents wanted to give him a special birthday weekend.

It didn't take long for Liberty to get ready. Once she had eaten dinner and done the washing up, she sat on the couch with a Bible on her lap and leaned back into the soft cushions behind her.

'What do you want to say to me today?' She closed her eyes and tilted her head heavenward.

After waiting in the Lord's presence for a couple of minutes, she opened her Bible to where she had left off the day before, and remembered that she had just finished the book of Job and was about to start the book of Psalms. As she read chapter 1, she took note of verse 3:

That person is like a tree planted by streams of water, which yields its fruit in season and whose leaf does not wither - whatever they do prospers.

Being planted by 'streams' of water stood out to her. 'It's not just one stream,' she thought, 'but many streams'. Liberty recalled the river of the water of life in Revelation 22, and considered that there is just one river, but many streams flow from it. Liberty wrote in her journal:

I can draw from the one river, by being planted by many streams. What are my streams? Devotional times, being regularly at church, close relationships, special times away with the Lord… and other connection points. These are like streams which cause me to yield fruit, keeps me from withering, and helps me to prosper.

Just then there was a knock on the door, and the sound of it opening, with the familiar voice of her friend Layla calling, "Hello, we're here."

"I'm in the lounge," Liberty called back as she closed her journal and jumped up to greet her friends. Layla threw her arms around Liberty as she entered the room with Trinity and Samantha following behind. They were glad to be together again, and especially on the one year anniversary of their epic mission.

"Caden will be here soon," said Layla. "He's just finished band practice, then picking up Tristan from the gym."

"Great!" Liberty responded. "How are things going at church? Any big events lined up?"

"Oh, there is always something going on," Layla answered with a smile. "We are hosting a pastors and leaders conference in a couple of weeks. We are gathering leaders from all over the region with some great guest speakers to share what God has for us at this time, and to release a fresh anointing. It's also a chance for our churches to hang out and build stronger relationships together."

'Layla is such a gifted leader and organiser,' thought Liberty, appreciating their developing friendship. Liberty and the other girls saw Layla as a kind of role-model, as Layla was a few years older than they were.

"Sounds amazing!" Liberty responded.

The boys arrived and were offered hot drinks, then the six gathered in the lounge.

"Awesome to have you all here. I'm so glad you could all make it!" announced Liberty.

"I wouldn't miss this for anything," said Trinity, who always loved being in on the action. "Our adventure was amazing. Would sooo love to do it again! Sam, you'd look great with another pair of wings, soaring into battle."

"Ha!" Samantha responded. "Would be wonderful to soar through the air again! And, I'd love to see Layla take out another demon with her bow, like that one on the throne. It had no chance against a lethal warrior princess!"

Layla smiled at her friends, "Oh, you are too kind! I'll always treasure our memories, and I'm so glad that we are all together to mark the occasion."

"Well, you never know what could happen, even tonight as we pray," replied Liberty.

"Might have some angels come and join us," said Caden with a laugh.

Samantha nudged Liberty with her elbow. "Wouldn't it be beautiful to be in the presence of angels again?"

"Okay, I lead off. Shall we be led by the Spirit, and see what happens?" Liberty asked.

"Perfect!" encouraged Layla.

Liberty began to pray, "Lord, we come to you tonight. We are here together in unity, under an open heaven, to glorify you, to lift you up, and to thank you for all that you have done. Thank you so much for using us to help save our city. What a privilege to be used by you, and to partner with you. Lord, fill us again by your Spirit, and help us to hear you tonight."

All six earnestly pressed in to seek the Lord and sensed the presence of the Holy Spirit start to fill the room.

Layla prayed, "Bring heaven to earth, show us more than we have seen."

Each had their eyes closed, trying to see with their spirit. As they did, a faint sparkling cloud started to form within the room. Their prayer caused the cloud to expand into a dome, stretching out until it completely enveloped them. Their unity welcomed the Lord's presence and power. Within the room glistening droplets started to fall, droplets of glory, washing away any doubts and insecurities and any sin from the day. Liberty could sense this in the spirit, but she opened her eyes hoping that she would be able to see the glory unfolding.

"It's happening," she said. "Can you see it?"

Each opened their eyes.

"Yes!" exclaimed Samantha in excitement. "I see the glory. It's like glistening rain!" and she lifted her hands to let the sparkles splash onto her palms.

The six looked around in wonder as the glory started to rain down harder. What had started as single droplets, quickly turned into a downpour. It was like being outside in very heavy rain, or like standing under a waterfall. Liberty held her arms out with palms up, and her mouth wide open and a look of wonder on her face.

"Look!" pointed Tristan. "Layla is disappearing!"

"Yes, she is," replied Trinity, "but so are you."

"We all are," said Caden. "It's like the rain is washing us away.

You're going transparent,' he said pointing back at Trinity.

Samantha also got the giggles, "You know what Caden?" she joked. "Sometimes I can just see right through you!"

"Ha-ha!" he responded.

Trinity burst out laughing, she couldn't help it. She waved with a huge grin. "See you!" And those were the last words that any of them got out before being completely washed away in the glory shower.

As the rain fell, the room faded away from sight, and the six were washed to another place.

Liberty watched the room dissolving away, disappearing into darkness. She strained her eyes to see anything, but all became dark. After some undetermined amount of time, she started to feel a breeze against her skin. As she kept her eyes open, she noticed little sparkles appearing way off in the distance.

'What are they?' she thought.

The longer she looked, the more her eyes were becoming accustomed to the darkness, and more lights appeared.

'Some of them are in rows,' she thought, as the scene around her got clearer. Rows of lights criss-crossed in front of her, and other lights were scattered about. Her surroundings were coming into focus and taking shape around her.

"Oh, it's Riverdale!" she exclaimed out loud.

The six materialised on a grassy clearing. Stepping forward toward the edge of the cliff, they found themselves overlooking Grace Falls against the stunning backdrop of Riverdale's cityscape. As they stood on the clifftop, another came and stood alongside them.

Caden looked across to his left "Jack!" he exclaimed.

"Hi team," he replied.

Then others joined them.

"Falcon!" said Liberty.

Seraph, Shar, and Trillion also appeared, along with the commissioning angel. The six were now twelve.

Liberty looked out surveying Riverdale, admiring the blue ribbon of light as it rose high up into the night sky. It ran down Grace Falls, making the water glisten, and followed the river as it flowed southwards. The red axis hung in the air over Razor Peak, and crossed the city from West to East. Where these intersected, was the bright golden axis that blazed upwards as a pillar of light. The city had remained gloriously in alignment.

"Are you ready?" said the commissioning angel.

"For what?" said Caden slowly, almost knowing what may come next.

"Your city is secure, but there are others," said the angel.

"Are we going on another adventure?" asked Trinity with a twinkle in her eye.

"Your fellowship was the first of its kind. Since then there have been others. But there is a city in desperate need, and we need your experience and faith on this mission. Will you accept the assignment to save another city that is appointed?"

The six looked at each other and couldn't help showing their excitement.

"I think we are all up for the challenge," replied Tristan. "Where are we going?"

"You will see," said the angel.

The twelve remained for a moment. Then, yet again, they found themselves being transported to another place.

The lights faded and the team dissolved out of earth-realm. A wind blew across the empty clifftop. Blades of grass quivered in the breeze. A puff of dust blew through the emptiness where the twelve had stood just moments before. Elsewhere across time and space, a team was about to be deployed into battle, but here, on this night, all was quiet, all was peace.

4

GATHERED

Riverdale faded away, and so did the silence. All around Liberty a muffled roaring sound was getting louder and louder until it filled her ears. It sounded a bit like... rushing water! Suddenly she was engulfed, thrust under water. Liberty flapped her arms and her hands broke the surface. She pushed up and gasped for breath. She shot downstream through the fast flowing river. Liberty glanced around, wide eyed trying to get her bearings. 'Where are the others?!' she thought.

At the mercy of the rushing water, she paddled hard to stay afloat. Suddenly Liberty saw a wall of water in front of her. She took a deep breath, then went under. She manoeuvred her body into a feet-first position with her arms spread out trying to keep steady. Liberty emerged from the water, and took another breath. She bobbed up and down in the rough rapids, endeavouring to keep her head above the surface, making the most of every breath. Again she got submerged as the current pulled her down, then released her to burst out of the water.

Liberty looked back and spotted Tristan and Layla up river, struggling to keep afloat like she was. She steadied her breathing and kept her arms out and allowed the river to take her to wherever it was taking her. It was only now that she noticed what was beyond the river banks. What she saw was amazing. Trees and fields whipped past. Then suddenly a city would rush by and she would catch a glimpse of buildings and parks and people going about their daily business. And again fields, and open spaces. Light came and went. Suddenly she was out at sea in the midst of a vast open expanse. Then back to civilization again. She glided quickly through towns and villages and rural settings. The people she momentarily caught sight of looked like from times past, lords, ladies, peasants…

After a while, she realised that she was in a semi-transparent tunnel. It was like looking through curved glass, a lens, slightly hazy, but clear enough to tell that she was going very fast, and going a very long way. Even though she could see all of her surroundings, she was aware that no one could look in to see her whisking past them, being swept downstream. Perhaps it was the speed, but more than likely, the tunnel was concealing the travellers who were within it.

As she neared a bend in the river, bringing her close to the river bank, she was suddenly yanked to the side and pulled out of the water. She let out a "Woah!" and found herself flung through the air and out of the river. She raised her arms to shield her head from being smashed against the glassy surface. Then out…

***

There was no impact of glass. Liberty looked down as she was flying through the air, and saw that she was about to hit the ground from quite a height. She stretched out her arms in preparation for a dive-roll, and gracefully broke her landing by rolling across her right shoulder, along her back, and then rolled up to her feet. Liberty spun to look behind to see her five friends emerging from the tunnel, flying through the air. Each broke their fall gracefully in dive-rolls, like seasoned athletes, or rather warriors, as each was now clothed in armour, suitably equipped to rescue a city from the forces of darkness.

The six stood still for a moment, gazing around their new surroundings. Where they stood was like nowhere they had ever been before. It was nothing like the landscape that they had been gliding through. Samantha spun around in amazement, "What a wonderful place!" she exclaimed.

They stood on an ancient open pavilion the size of a football field. The polished marble surface reflected the star-systems that dazzled from the skies above. Embedded into the floor were metal strips that splayed out from the centre like markers indicating directions to other parts of the universe. Encompassing the edges of the pavilion were giant pillars, five on each side. The twenty foot pillars supported a thick stone trim that followed the edge of the pavilion. With no roof, the trim framed the starry expanse above.

The six looked around in wonder trying to take it all in. 'I feel like I'm so high up, but not above the ground, more like above creation,' thought Liberty. The pavilion was set on the top of an enormous mountain that floated in space. But it wasn't just one mountain, there were mountains on mountains, forming one gargantuan pinnacle that was a vantage point for the universe.

Then a glow appeared in space. The light quickly drew nearer. As it reached the far end of the pavilion, it arrested everyone's attention. It came with its own atmosphere, its own weather pattern. Darkness was a canopy around it, and storm clouds advanced overhead. Then out of the brightness, it started to take the shape of a person. The details of its form became sharp and Liberty recognised it as being an angel. This angel wore armour that glowed with a scorching heat. Its moulded plates looked like they had been cast at a million degrees in the heart of a star. His arms and legs were like liquid fire, blazing like a raging furnace. Liberty could see his fingers, and could imagine that he had run them through the gasses of forming stars during creation, stirring them along into life. He was probably one who had stood in the centre of the universe at the dawn of time, and plunged his arms into the depths of the molten elements, spinning them into fiery discs and forming spiral galaxies. He would have drawn out bright balls of liquid and cast them across space to separate out the constellations.

The air around him distorted, like a curtain being blown in a breeze. His presence couldn't be held securely in this reality because he was from a different one. Realities beyond realities. Liberty was amazed at his appearance. She noticed thin wisps of lightning around him forming geometric patterns. She saw fading hexagons, bursts of triangles, and spirals flaming into existence, and then fading into nothingness. The elements within the atmosphere around him were being torn apart as mathematical equations and laws holding the universe together were dissolving in his presence. Reality ruptured and burst around him. Each particle, element and law, displaying its own signature, lasted for a moment, before being undone. The hard marble floor beneath his feet creased and wrinkled as matter distorted under him. He walked toward them.

The angel then spoke in a voice that echoed with authority. "You are standing on one of the Pinnacles of Knowledge," he said. The vapour from his breath glistened in the light.

'One of the Pinnacles of Knowledge?' thought Liberty to herself. 'I wonder how many are there.'

"There are countless," responded the angel smiling.

'Oh God, he can read my thoughts!' said Liberty to herself, now trying to think of absolutely nothing… but failing miserably.

"You have been called to one of our meeting points to be briefed on your next mission," the angel continued.

'Wow, our next mission,' thought Liberty, realising that it was going to be impossible for her to think of completely nothing. 'What a privilege to be caught up again in the epic saga between light and darkness.'

Trinity voiced her thoughts, "Is this a part of heaven?"

"Good question," said the angel who was graciously waiting for the humans to ask the questions that he would have answered anyway even had they not been asked. "This is a place in the spirit realm, but it is not heaven. Jesus does have dominion here and throughout every realm, but his city is far from these mountains. This is simply a place we can meet to find knowledge in a secure location. Here we are unhindered by the enemy. No demon passes through here. It is too high."

"Do other humans come to this place?" asked Layla.

"Very few angels have even been here. The realms are vast and humans see very little of what is. But this mountain has been set aside for us."

Layla felt honoured and also amazed at how expansive God is.

'There is so much more than we could ever know,' she thought.

"The earth stands at an important time," said the angel who now got to the point, having given the humans long enough to adjust to their surroundings. "You are being sent to bring alignment to triaxial identifiers, like you did in Riverdale. You now understand that each city has an altar, a throne and an atmosphere and how these must be aligned for the purposes and blessings of God to flow. But this time you will be fighting for a different city, not your own."

"What's the city?" asked Tristan.

"The city you have been assigned to is Geneva," the angel responded.

"Geneva! You mean the city over in France?" inquired Tristan.

"Switzerland actually," Trinity corrected.

"Isn't Geneva the headquarters of the United Nations?" asked Caden turning toward Trinity.

"That is yet to be decided," responded the angel.

'Yet to be decided?!' thought Trinity. 'Geneva is arguably one of the most important cities in the world!' she thought. Trinity had spent a lot of time studying the history of Geneva for a school project, and also studied its contribution to global diplomacy and financial services.

Then she heard her thoughts being spoken out loud, "The Geneva Convention written in 1949, and it outlines humanitarian rights during times of conflict… Am I thinking this or saying this?..."

"Switzerland also happens to be the richest country in the world, with the highest average per-capita wealth. Geneva also manages around 50% of all private wealth, and has been ranked as one of the highest quality of life countries. Switzerland is also known for precision and integrity including watch-making."

"Thank you," said the angel.

"What?!" said Trinity. "Did you guys hear what I was just thinking?"

"I felt it important for everyone to hear your thoughts," responded the angel.

Feeling slightly embarrassed, Trinity was aware that her school project was probably a little less important than the mission that they were about to be given. She usually had something to say for most occasions, but she started to blush realising that she was effectively butting in on a once in a lifetime address from a glorious and powerful angel who probably had all knowledge and understanding.

"Very good," said the angel reassuring her. "But none of that has happened yet."

"Hasn't happened yet?!" protested Trinity who again couldn't help herself.

"What you don't realise," explained the angel, "is that not only have you crossed from the surface to the spirit realm, you have also travelled to another location on the globe, and you have all traversed across time."

Layla looked across to Liberty and mouthed 'Wow!" They all looked at each other with big smiles. Not only were they navigating new realms and places, but were also now time travellers.

"The river that we lifted you out of is a time passage. You have travelled back through time for this next mission. Although, from an earth time point of view, this is your first mission. Your Riverdale mission will be in about 500 years," he said with a slight smile.

"The earth date is 14 January 1537. Prayer has been lifted up, to give us the ability to see the city and your quest. I will now show you

Geneva, as it is at this time." The angel extended his arm with his palm raised, and slowly drew it across the sky. As he did, the scene before them changed.

As Liberty and the team looked, the spiritual landscape of Geneva materialised in front of them. The compass of John's prayer surrounded the city, with the golden sweeping arcs moving overhead.

Samantha gasped, "The city is devastated!" Immediately she began to choke up and her eyes began to water moved by the destruction of the ruined city. Stone and brick buildings looked more like stalagmites than engineered architectural structures. "The city is already without any hope," she muttered.

"Yes, that's how some see it," said the angel.

"Oh, how could it be like this?" asked Samantha, who felt the heaviness of the destruction in her heart.

"Cities are not always as they seem. It depends on your vantage point," said the angel. "For many, this is the reality of the city, but have you ever noticed how two people can be looking at the same thing, but see something totally different?"

"Like a glass, half empty and half full at the same time?" suggested Caden.

"Exactly. Let me show you," said the angel.

The angel raised both hands in a large arc and crossed his hands over as he brought them down in a sweeping motion. The ground beneath Liberty slid sideways. Liberty looked down to see that they were standing around the edge of the compass which was sliding beneath them. The buildings began to move, as their journey around the city commenced. Liberty held her stomach feeling a little motion sick as she was lurched sideways. All was in motion and made her feel like she was out at sea, with nothing stationary around her. The team began to orbit the city.

Wind whipped at Liberty's hair so she tucked it behind her ear. As shadows shifted around the city, an amazing transformation took place as they watched. The city was rebuilding itself. They eventually got halfway around the city, to a vantage point on the opposite side to the one they started on. By that time the city had rebuilt itself and was completely restored. But they continued their trajectory around the city, and it began to degenerate again.

The angel half shouted so that they could hear him, as the team continued their journey "The appearance of the city is both in good shape and a ruin. You have just been given a collective perspective of the people who live here. Some people see God at work everywhere and the city looks in good health to them. Others see only the negative, and everything looks hopeless. The actual state of the city is seen only through the eyes of God, understanding the times and the seasons and knowing how he is at work. No single person has a perfect perspective. The ones with the best perspective are those who ask for the Lord's vision, and who also have many relationships across the city. Those who reach out to every level of society, and listen to what people are saying, are able to gain a clearer picture of the city's life-stage.

"One of the greatest keys to clarity of vision is relationships. You can't see clearly without meaningful relationships, and you can't even fulfil the call of God for your life without relationships. Each person sees a glimpse of God's plans through the relationships that they have, like peering through a doorway that is slightly open. In a multitude of counsellors there is wisdom."

Liberty thought of a sports game on a field, with multiple camera angles needed to make a well informed call on a play. One camera may have a better angle for some plays, but many cameras are needed for the entire game."

The six stood in awe as they viewed the city before them being constructed and deconstructed in front of them.

Caden was first to notice, and yelled out, "I can faintly see the tri-axial identifiers running through the city."

"Yes. These are only empty constructs of what will be once you set them up," the angel called back. "You will each have a path to follow to fulfil your mission. Caden and Tristan red. Layla, Samantha, and Trinity blue. Liberty gold." The six looked hard at their own colour, doing their best to get a feel for where they would be travelling. Seeing a map in advance of where they would be going, made it more personal and real for each of them. Their next quest was about to begin.

5

ASSIGNMENTS

"You have been given two days to win the altar, the throne, and the atmosphere for Geneva," the angel informed them. "You have only two days because any more than that would give the enemy time to build their forces against you. As it is, they are unaware of your existence in this time, but once you step out into your mission, your presence will be felt."

The team could see the tri-axial identifiers of the altar, the throne, and the atmosphere in front of them within the city-wide compass and rotating gyroscopes.

"Caden and Tristan, your mission will be the atmosphere."

"Like last time," said Tristan with a smile, and gave Caden a nudge.

"Not quite," said the angel. "The Elemental Stone has yet to be set up at this point in history. Your goal is to establish the Elemental Stone to influence the atmosphere of the city."

"How do we set it up?"

"The atmosphere of the city is always set up through prayer. There have been a small group of Christians who have been praying for this city for many years. In two days, they are meeting at the village of Choulex. You will be heading east, to clear the path for them so that they can get to that location. The culmination of their prayers have almost reached critical mass and though they don't know it, this gathering will release the breakthrough, and set up the Elemental Stone for Geneva and this region of the world. This stone will have a far greater influence than many stones set up in other places. This stone will set up an axis that will circumnavigate the whole globe as a reference point for centuries to come."

'Oh wow,' thought Caden, 'I thought saving Riverdale was big. This is massive!'

"The two of you will be dropped at different locations, and will each need to protect the person that you have been individually assigned to. Make sure they reach their destination."

'We got this!' thought Tristan.

"Tristan, your assignment will be Haans for these next two days. Protect him, and clear the path for him. He is in good hands with you," the angel added, giving Tristan an encouraging wink.

"Caden, you will be protecting Pierre who owns two businesses, and on a number of committees within the city. It is important that you guard Pierre well. The enemy has many tricks, but you can complete your quest if you maintain faith, and rely on the Holy Spirit to provide you with discernment."

The angel then turned to the girls.

"Layla, Samantha, and Trinity, you are to secure the throne. The throne has already been established, but demonic forces have brought chaos and have set up their own rule around the throne. You will be heading northward toward Lake Geneva. The throne is out on the lake within Crystal City. But it is too exposed to drop you out on the lake. The enemy will feel the displacement of your arrival. So you will be dropped some distance away at a safe location, and you will make your way to the water's edge."

'Sounds like we have a journey on our hands. Can't wait to start!' thought Trinity with a smile.

"Liberty, yours is the altar. Secure the keys, claim the altar, set up the triaxial identifier, and all within two days before the meeting of the Grand Council."

"Had a feeling I'd be alone again," mumbled Liberty.

"Yes, you have a solo mission, but you will not be alone, you will have help from Falcon and other angels."

The commissioning angel paused, then said, "There is something about your mission that I cannot see yet. I cannot see how you will achieve your goal because the keys seem to inevitably fall into enemy hands."

'Well that's good!' thought Liberty. 'A failed quest before I start!'

"You are here for a reason," said the angel in response. "You must try. You wouldn't be here if there was no hope, so one way or another you must find the hidden pathway of success. You will need faith and also people praying for you on the surface."

"Do you mean friends back home praying? Like from the future, where we're from?" asked Liberty.

"Yes. Prayer cannot alter the past, but people can pray specifically for you because you don't belong to this time. For the success of this mission you will need the prayers of people praying for you back home, and also the prayers of people from this time.

"You will be dropped in the heart of the city close to the vault," said the angel.

"Is the vault where the keys are? How do I find the keys once I'm there?" Liberty asked.

"When you land, you will see a man with a long jacket, a walking cane, and a chequered cloth hat. Follow him. He will lead you to the vault where keys should be stored. Once you are there, you can use this medallion to unlock the appropriate safety deposit box."

The angel handed Liberty a star-shaped medallion. She wondered how many boxes she would have to try before finding the one box that the medallion fitted into to release the keys. She tucked it away in a side pocket on her thigh.

"That is all we have time for. All is set in motion. You will now be released and may the Lord be with you," said the angel with a solemn look.

With that the fiery angel looked up and raised his arms. As he did, a beam of light shot up into the heavens. Streams of power spiralled around him. Then he swept his arms down and out, beams of light splayed out around him. Suddenly the team was separated, forced away in various directions.

Caden and Tristan were pushed backwards toward one end of the pavilion. It happened so fast that all the boys could do was look at each other with wide open eyes. Caden spun around to see the approaching edge of the pavilion, then disappeared between two pillars in a burst of fiery sparks. Embers skipped across the shiny floor. Tristan also turned to face the approaching edge. Suddenly there was another flash of sparks accompanied by crackling sounds. Fiery sparks flew everywhere.

The girls were forced back in a different direction. Samantha reached out for Trinity's hand and gripped it hard as the three girls were steered toward the opposite perimeter, then dropped off the edge. Trinity and Samantha were still holding hands as they went into freefall, picking up speed as the wind whipped past them. Layla felt relaxed enough to allow the force to push her back, trusting that no harm would come to her. Suddenly her stomach jumped into her mouth as she fell backwards over the edge and went into freefall. Looking up, she saw the pavilion very quickly getting smaller and smaller as she plummeted through the air. Then, in mid-air, all three girls suddenly vanished, long before hitting the landscape far below.

Liberty was forced back in another direction. She saw the boys disappear as they reached the edge. She saw the girls fall, and wondered what would happen to her. Liberty spun around to face the end of the pavilion that was fast approaching. Without knowing why exactly, perhaps simply embracing the moment, she ran forward and jumped as she got to the rim. She drew her arms straight out in front of her and dived off the pavilion into empty space. There was not the same gravitational effect on Liberty as there had been on the other girls. She soared into space. There was no noise; the silence between worlds.

Looking down, she could see mountain ranges protruding through pockets of cloud-cover. The ranges were vast. Snow dusted the tops of the higher ranges. Forests and lakes and rivers covered the midlands. Sandy, barren deserts spread out across the lower territories. Out ahead of her were stars upon stars. She continued to glide out into space, floating on the force from the angel. Still in horizontal free-fall, Liberty rolled over and her vision was filled with galaxies and stars.

One large galaxy was particularly close, dressing the sky above. The bright orange arms with a red outer glow arced around the brilliant centre, forming a sparkling disc of billions of stars. Then all the beauty and glory around her began to darken. Liberty felt lighter, like she was being dispersed into particles.

'I'm leaving,' she thought as her body was translated from this place to another.

This visit to an outer realm pavilion was at an end. A new realm was about to open up. There would be many challenges to overcome, and victories to achieve.

6

LANDING

- mission liberty -

Liberty landed on a cobblestone pavement next to a timber-framed building. She ran her hand along one of the smooth wooden beams. The dark interlocking beams formed geometric patterns, and white plaster filled in the sections of the wall. She pressed herself against it to draw as little attention to herself as possible, while getting a bearing of her surroundings.

A young couple walking arm in arm came up from behind her and brushed past, giving her a fright. They didn't see her, as they continued on in light conversation, but she felt them go by.

She followed them with her eyes, admiring the fashion of the 1500's. The lady wore a full-length dress with red and white vertical stripes. Over the top she wore a light green cropped jacket with puffy sleeves, a bonnet, and carrying a wicker basket over one arm, with wild flowers neatly placed inside. The young man wore a long brown jacket which reached half way down his legs, exposing his long white tights and black shoes. Under his jacket was a red waistcoat, finished with a black scarf around his neck and a black hat that was turned up on either side towards the front to give it a triangular shape.

'I wonder if they would be able to feel me if I stretched my arm out?' she thought. But she didn't want to try.

Liberty looked around, and all was a buzz of activity. She found herself in a bustling town, with townsfolk going about their daily business, and children running along the street. There were horses and carts, people carrying boxes of goods, sellers, and also those having casual conversations outside shops, and on street corners.

She then noticed a couple of dark figures following an elderly man as he crossed the road. She also became aware of a creature circling in the sky above. Then across the road there were four other demons talking and pointing in the direction of a group of people.

'I better be careful,' thought Liberty. 'Even though the people can't see me, I bet the demons can.'

She remained in her position for a while, scanning the crowds, looking out for a man with a chequered cloth hat, walking cane and long jacket. There were a number of men wearing single-coloured, short-brimmed hats; some with a feather or foliage sticking out of the side of them. A number had woven straw hats, neatly finished with a black fabric band around the crown. Some men had walking canes, but none matched the description of having the particular hat, the cane and the jacket. Liberty remained patient, listing to the clomping of shoes on the pavement and the rolling of wooden cartwheels along the cobblestones.

A few minutes later, she spotted a man in the crowd wearing a hat with stitching that made it look chequered and long jacket.

'Nope, doesn't appear to have a cane,' she thought, as he crossed the road walking away from her.

"Hold on, he does!" she exclaimed to herself, as she saw him tap the wheel of a carriage with his cane as it went past him. She hadn't noticed the cane before because he was holding it in his right hand, on the opposite side to her.

Liberty immediately got up to follow, but then noticed some more demons walking in the same direction.

'Nuts! How am I going to get through all of this unnoticed?' she thought. The man continued to get further away from her. 'If I don't move now, I'll lose him in the crowd.'

Liberty went to move, but noticed another demon on top of a building looking down at the busy intersection. She held back. Liberty was getting desperate. Droplets of sweat appeared on her forehead.

"Lord, give me a path," she prayed as she brushed her hair back. Suddenly she saw a group of five women loudly talking together about their children's schooling and family matters.

Over the street noise she could hear, "It's washing day today, and all three of my children are at home helping out," said one lady loudly.

"Lucky you! My boys are off with their friends somewhere. I never know where they are, then they suddenly appear at dinner time. It's amazing!" said a woman beside her.

"Then maybe you should serve them up a pile of washing on their dinner plates! They can eat real food once the pile has disappeared," said a third laughing.

"You know what? I'm going to do just that!" she responded.

'That's my cover,' Liberty thought, and quickly moved from her position to walk beside the group of ladies, trying to stay out of the view of the demon on the roof. The ladies continued walking and talking and remained good cover until they were getting too far away from where she wanted to go. Liberty sidled up to another group walking in the same direction, but she needed to move fast and get across the road. Walking quickly she looked for her opportunity. A group of children burst onto the road chasing a puppy who was in turn chasing a rat. Liberty sprung forward, and ran next to the taller ones, while trying to keep the man with the chequered hat in sight. She could still see him, and managed to cover good ground, keeping him in her sights. She sidled up to another building staying close to it.

'So good, so far,' she whispered to herself, and continued to stealthily follow.

Just then the sky above them darkened as a shadow reached across the area where they were, like a passing cloud covering the sun. Liberty quickly manoeuvred herself behind a couple of stalls. She was now getting quite close to him.

Then a voice shouted from the crowd, "Hey John, over here." The man in the chequered hat snapped out of deep thought, looked up and smiled at the one addressing him. He started his way over towards the direction of the one who had called his name.

'Okay, so his name is John – normal name,' thought Liberty.

As she looked towards the one who had called him over, she got a fright when she saw five demons standing behind the group of men.

'Something bad is going to happen,' thought Liberty. 'Do I remain concealed, or do I defend my assignment?'

'Defend,' immediately came to mind.

'A Holy Spirit thought, or just my own idea?... No time to wait. It's happening now. Need to step out in faith.'

Liberty started to jog toward John. As he got to the group, one of the demons stepped forward and clawed at him. Suddenly John scrunched his eyes and held his head like having a sudden headache. He dropped to his knees. Two of the men quickly came to either side of him to help him up, asking if he was alright. The men could not see what Liberty could.

As the demon was about to claw him again, Liberty rushed forward, raised her sword, and swung it over the top of John's head. The demon reeled back in surprise. Liberty went for the demon again, but it raised its own sword and defended the attack. The clang of blades prompted the other demons in the group to lift their weapons.

'Oh no,' thought Liberty. 'I'm attracting too much attention. Maybe a bad move to engage so soon, but now it's 'game on'!' Liberty spun and sliced through the air, knocking the sword from the demon's hand. She lunged forward, and drove her sword through her enemy. Liberty side-stepped John and cut through two more demons to her left. As a demon on her right tried to engage her, she sent a back-kick to its head, and it dropped to the ground. The battle intensified as more demons nearby descended on her. Liberty knocked back demon after demon, displaying skilful swordsmanship. Despite her competent attack, she found herself surrounded. Staying light on her feet, she stepped up onto a cart, and jumped across to swing on a sign keeping out of reach of the assault.

As she landed on the ground, she saw an angel walking toward her to join the battle. He was covered in brilliant white feathers. As he walked, the sunlight slipped down its silky attire. Dirt and dust slid right off his feathers, with no way to cling to this magnificent creature. He held a clear shield, and was adorned with diamond armour. He drew near, and unsheathed a glassy sword. As he did, each feather on his body flipped over, revealing a black underside. Suddenly, the creature whom she thought represented heaven's armies, was transformed into a dark lord, with oily black feathers and a foreboding presence. His armour and shield clouded over, becoming a graphite grey.

Liberty turned to run, but two demons were in her way, so she darted to her right. Liberty leapt up the wall of a building, taking a couple of side steps on the wall, and pushed off into a flip and swung her sword, banishing the two from the realm. An arrow was fired by a demon with a crossbow from the roof. She ducked, narrowly avoiding being shot. The dark lord continued to walk toward her, as Liberty faced it, breathing hard.

***

Back in Riverdale, Sierra was working on her second album 'Beyond the Storm'. Her first album had been successful with two of her songs in the top 10 charts. The 'Reborn' tour had sold out venues all over the country and her fan base was steadily growing. Her social media manager continued to keep the fans happy with regular posts from the tour, along with music clips, candid shots of Sierra talking to fans, and backstage insights.

Being on tour with her team had been an amazing experience, and one she wanted to do again, but first she needed a decent break from being on the road for two months. Back home again, it was time to come up with new content, new lyrics, new rifts, reflecting the theme of her new album. The songs were about having strong and courageous faith, overcoming darkness, and living the victorious faith-filled life, filled with the Holy Spirit. Sierra wanted 'Beyond the

Storm' to build on her last album. If 'Reborn' was about finding life and finding faith, then 'Beyond the Storm' would be about living that life victoriously every day.

Sierra swung open the doors of her downtown Riverdale studio and dropped her handbag on the couch. Walking across to the kitchenette she got a mug to make herself a green tea. As the kettle was boiling, she looked around the modern studio with brick walls, adorned with art and posters, that inspired her creativity. Being on the fifth floor gave her a great view of downtown, including the river and the park across the road which was often busy with locals buying their morning coffee, and tourists exploring the city.

With her tea in one hand and pen and paper in the other, she sat down at her elegant and tidy desk, ready to work on one of her new songs 'We Are Here'.

We are here holy, set apart fire in our breath
Thunder in our heart
Beyond shadows of the night
Stepping into breaking light
We rise up in faith
Refined by fire
This life we live for you
We are taking higher and higher

'It's feeling good!' she thought. As Sierra wrote, her friend Liberty flashed in her mind and she felt an urgency to pray. 'Oh yes, 'prayer', this song needs to be more about prayer'. She rewrote a couple of lines…

We rise up in prayer
United in fire
This life we live for you
We are taking higher and higher

"That's better," she said, as the creativity continued to flow. Again the thought of Liberty flashed into her mind.

"Well, I'm writing about prayer. I had better do some. Lord wherever Liberty is right now, I pray that you would bless her, fill her with your Spirit. Give her wisdom and courage and power to fulfil your purposes and to give her victory."

As Sierra prayed, her prayer-form started to fill the room with a gentle hum. As she continued to pray the hum intensified and started to vibrate the spiritual fabric of the studio.

"Heavenly Father, you are in control of all things, all things bow at your command. I declare a blessing over Liberty. Wash away the enemies plans and make straight paths for her feet."

The audio groundswell increased in volume, creating translucent waves in the room, distorting the atmosphere like heat rising off a road on a hot summer's day. A large wave of visual sound developed around her. It swelled and crested, then suddenly broke releasing its power as it crashed outwards in all directions, breaking into millions of sparkling diamonds.

This was not just her prayer-form, but also was the 'Sierra anointing' that she carried. Her anointing not only rocked the spirit realm when she prayed, but also rocked stadiums when she played. The sound of her voice and her guitar would build a hum that resonated with what the Holy Spirit wanted to do. As the hum built into waves, they would be released and roll around the stadiums bringing deliverance and freedom. The waves would then break over people in a shower of diamonds, releasing hope and inspiration. This happened whenever she was involved in any kind of ministry.

The breaking waves in the studio where she was praying, showered diamonds all around her, and washed up the walls. They splayed out forcefully in all directions and then faded out, sent to another part of the spirit realm.

***

Liberty pulled back from the dark lord, to give herself a little more time and space to place her next advance.

'The other demons are not going to miss this fight!' she thought. Liberty was right. As she glanced around, more demons in the vicinity rushed toward her. From the tops of buildings they came. Those on assignments against the townsfolk broke off from their primary engagements to join the attack.

"It's all on now," Liberty said as she stood ready for the next wave of attack. With raised blade, ready for the onslaught from any direction, she noticed a hum starting to rise and reverberate around her.

Then suddenly a rush of sound propelled her forward toward the black towering creature. She flowed with the force, and quickly pushed off the ground raising her arms above her head, holding her sword with both hands. In mid-air, Liberty swung her sword, and an array of sharp, sparkling diamonds sprayed out from her blade. The diamonds fanned out, slashing three demons apart at once, but the dark lord defended itself with its large shield. As she brought her sword through the air again, millions of prayer propelled diamonds were released, which ripped apart other demons in the vicinity.

"Wow, I didn't know it could do that!" said Liberty.

Then the sound of the noise rose again, and a wall of diamonds materialised. The wave towered above Liberty, with the spray raining down glitter and diamonds. Demons from all over were running toward the scene. But as the wave broke, they were hit by the tremendous force of the gushing diamonds. The wave smothered the enemy, tearing through countless numbers of them. Liberty saw the dark lord get thrown backwards as it was engulfed in the crashing wave. The enemy horde disintegrated into millions of tiny pieces as the diamonds ripped through the streets.

Liberty remained in an attack stance, looking around to see what enemies remained. The waves continued to flow around her, with diamonds splashing against the walls of the buildings. She noticed other demons in the vicinity being enveloped and swept away by the prayer waves. Liberty looked up and saw that the flying demon had not been touched by the waves and was slowly flapping away into the distance.

"Great," said Liberty. "Just what I need. A tell-tale demon, off to alert another squadron of darkness."

The rumbling sound subsided as the sea of diamonds drained away, swirling around her boots. She found herself standing in front of the men helping John regain his composure. It felt a little unnerving standing in full sight of the men. She was of course invisible to them, but she could see them quite literally in front of her.

John got up.

"Are you alright?" asked one of the men.

"Yes, I'm fine. Don't know what happened. A sudden pain, but it's gone now."

"Careful Calvin, you should probably get a doctor's check-up."

"Yes, I'm probably due for one." He squeezed out a smile.

'Calvin?' thought Liberty. 'I thought his name was John.'

Then it dawned on her. 'Could this be John Calvin, who led a reformation of the church in the 1500's? Have I actually come back to help him?!'

Liberty decided it would be best to follow again from a distance in case any new demons emerged. But now she felt the added pressure of time. 'Who knows how long I have before being inundated with demons again? But the diamonds were pretty awesome. Love to know who prayed for me,' she thought with a smile.

Just as she turned to take cover against a nearby building, she nearly bumped into a young boy about 10 years old, who was looking up at her wide-eyed.

'What?!' thought Liberty, as she looked at him. He was looking right back.

"Can you see me?" she asked. The boy nodded. "How can you see me, you are just a boy." The boy continued to stare.

"Answer me!" said Liberty, putting her hands on her hips.

"Yes, I can see you. I can see all of you," said the boy.

"What do you mean 'all of us'? Do you mean the demons?" asked Liberty.

He nodded.

"Just so we are clear, the demons weren't 'with' me, and I am not a demon. In fact, I've killed some."

"I know," he said.

"So let me get this straight. You can see me and you can see demons? Have you always been able to see them?" Liberty inquired.

"Yes, and angels," said the boy.

"Oh. Are there any around here?" asked Liberty.

"No, not recently," the boy said.

"Oh okay. So you're a Christian then?" Liberty asked.

"No, I'm not a Christian. I don't come from a Christian family," the boy replied.

Liberty was intrigued, but also in a hurry and did not want to lose her assignment.

"Look," she said, "I don't have much time, I need to leave, but you really need to meet John Calvin and have a conversation with him."

"I know where John preaches, at the local church. I've just never been there. My mum thinks he is a strange man with funny ideas. I have never been to any church," he said.

"Do me a favour. One way or another, you need to get to church and listen to him preach because you need to understand that Jesus Christ died on the cross for you, to save you from your sins, and give you eternal life. It is the most important message you will ever hear. Oh, and by the way I'm Liberty, and what's your name?"

"I'm Alex, short for Alexander," he said, holding out his hand. Liberty went to shake hands and was slightly freaked that her hand went through his. Alex was also surprised.

"Anyway, I need to go," said Liberty, nice to meet you.

"Nice to meet you too," said Alex. "I like your armour," he said with a smile.

Liberty gave him a wink, and turned to follow John.

7

THE FALL
- MISSION TRISTAN -

Haans coughed. He then leaned back in his chair and took a deep breath and coughed deeply again clearing his throat and chest. He swallowed and leaned forward resuming his project, humming a melody as he worked. Wood chips flaked off around him and covered the ground like fresh snowfall.

His grey hair resembled a wire brush wrapped around his head. He wore a brown leather waistcoat and a cream shirt with sleeves rolled up bearing his strong forearms, and large worn hands. The wooden block he was holding was being crafted by the hands of a master craftsman. What once could have been left to rot in a forest, unseen by any human eye, was now being shaped into something that would be treasured. This toy would hold the centre of someone's attention for hours and hours.

***

Flickering sparks burst all around Tristan. It was like being in the middle of the fountain of sparks of a gigantic firework. The sparkles then reduced in intensity, and a room materialised around him.

The room was filled with all sorts of wooden crafts. The shelves around the walls were stacked with toys and models, along with tools hanging off pegs all neatly arranged. There were models of houses, boats and carts, along with figures and puppets. On the far wall hung two wooden shields and swords, perfect for young aspiring soldiers. Next to them in the corner, was a full sized pram that had been exquisitely crafted. Above the main entrance door was a carved sign which read 'Haans' Workshop'. In the middle of the room was a large wooden bench with various tools laid out, and sitting at the workbench was Haans himself, absorbed in his creativity.

'So all I have to do,' thought Tristan, 'is watch this guy work on projects, and make sure he gets to wherever he needs to be in a couple of days. Oh well, I had better get comfortable.'

In the corner, was a wooden rocking chair so Tristan walked over to it and tried to sit but found he couldn't. It was only then that he noticed what was getting in the way. A bow had materialised over one shoulder and a quiver full of arrows was slung over the other. He drew out an arrow and ran his fingers over the point, along the shaft, and over the feathers. Then he tried to bend it in his hands, testing his strength against the arrow.

'Yeah, I could snap it,' he thought. 'Better not.'

He adjusted the quiver, then he settled back into the chair, 'Could be a long wait,' he thought. As he sat, he spun the arrow in his fingers, then started to tap it on the floor, allowing it to bounce back in his hand.

***

Above him, two figures peered in through the window. Their large yellow eyes glanced around, and then disappeared again. The two scouts dropped down onto the ground outside the workshop and reported what they saw.

"What! A human has been assigned to him!" said Cretons grumpily, who had been awaiting their return.

"Haans must be more important than we thought," said Nash.

"Get reinforcements," Cretons responded. "Angels are one thing, but humans on assignment means that we are onto something big. We must take Haans out of the game, but we'll have to deal with the other human first."

"At least we know how to get rid of Haans," said Belrog with crafty intent.

More demons flapped in to join the gathering, which had now become a dozen.

Cretons spoke up, "Abaddon, you find whatever infirmity spirits are available, and get them over to Haans, and dump whatever you can on him. He won't last long."

Abaddon had tusks like a boar that protruded from his lower jaw. Its patchwork of leather armour concealed its muscular figure. The demon stood tall, and was well equipped to carry out its assignments, and do damage against its enemies.

"Consider it done," responded Abaddon. With that, it turned and sprinted off quickly to recruit the infirmity spirits.

Cretons, who was giving the orders, turned to another creature who was standing beside him.

"Gazgoul, get your band of punks over there and drop the human. We need him gone. I don't care if you perish while doing it.

Just eliminate the interference."

Gazgoul snarled and motioned with its head, beckoning some of the other demons to follow.

***

Meanwhile Tristan had been admiring Haans as he worked, while still spinning the arrow between his fingers and tapping it on the floor. Every so often Haans coughed needing to clear his throat.

Suddenly Tristan heard a cracking of floorboards beneath him. "What's that?!" he said, as he looked down at the floor. One side of the rocking chair dropped through a floorboard. Tristan remained sitting a few seconds longer while the chair was on an angle, with part of it through the floor. Then there was another crack. The chair jolted again. Then in an instant, Tristan disappeared through the hole that had opened up beneath him. He clawed at the sides of the pit as he fell, and spread his legs to slow his descent. With the arrow still in his hand, he plunged it into the earth. Instantly the arrow shot out front and back to the size of a javelin, and firmly embedded itself into the dirt and rock. Tristan was jolted as he came to an abrupt stop, desperately trying to hang on with both hands. Showers of dirt fell around him as he hung. One hand slid off, but he managed to bring it up again and hold tight. He was now breathing hard.

The sudden fall and the abrupt stop had left him feeling shaken. But both hands now had a firm grasp of the arrow, while his legs were hanging above the darkness. He looked up and saw the small jagged circle of light a long way above him. There was nothing he could do, just hang in mid-air. The air was stuffy and smelt old. 'What happened?!' Tristan thought. 'How do I get myself out of this mess?'

Suddenly the light above was obstructed by two figures peering down at him.

Then, from below, was the sound of chatter and the scurrying of claws.

"No!" said Tristan. "Demons above and below!"

The demons above dropped into the shaft to attack him. All Tristan could do was to let go. He instinctively drew an arrow and shot upwards. The arrow pierced both demons that were descending toward him. Tristan fell onto a demon below. Now all were plummeting towards the bottom. Immediately Tristan reached for the knife secured to his thigh, drew it out, and thrust it downwards into the body below him. The demon roared. He felt a second jolt as they fell onto another demon lower down. It made a swipe at him, trying to reach past the first as they were falling. The swipe of its claws glanced off Tristan's armour. Tristan drew another arrow and shot downwards. This arrow hit its mark and the demon burst into flame. Just then his body smashed onto the ground hard thud, and they all came crashing down on top of each other. An explosion of flame filled the cavern. The two demons below Tristan broke his fall as he rolled away. As the ones from above came crashing down on top of the pile in another ball of flame that lit up the cavern. Unaware of how many there were, Tristan immediately drew another arrow and spun around to look in every direction. Fortunately the pile of four burning demons gave off enough light to illuminate his surroundings.

Tristan heard a snarl and turned to see demon dogs about to attack. Tristan knew he was in real danger, but an inward confidence kept his mind sharp. He shot the first dog, but then another jumped on to his back. He reached behind and flung it off, reloaded another arrow and shot. Again a 'fire arrow' caused an explosion of light. Unwilling to be jumped on again from behind, Tristan ran to one end of the cavern and skidded behind a rock. At least now his attackers would only come at him from one direction. Breathing hard and ready to fight, Tristan loaded another arrow at the ready to shoot again.

Two large demons emerged from the far side of the cavern carrying some kind of device. A smaller demon said, "He's over there!" pointing toward Tristan. The two demons drew closer, raising the device they were carrying between them. "Get away!" yelled one of the demons, at the pack of dogs that were hanging back snarling at Tristan.

"That's far enough," said one, and dropped the object down between them. Without further warning, a loud bang sent a heavy net flying toward Tristan. It splayed out like a star-shaped spider's web with claws surrounding the edges. Then, with a thud, it engulfed Tristan and the rock he was hiding behind, and held fast to the rock wall of the cavern. Fortunately with the rock in front offered some protection and breathing room.

Tristan raised his bow and shot at one of the large demons through the web. But it raised the device deflecting the arrow, and grazing the one standing beside.

"Owww" screamed the demon. "Stand back. Get out of range!"

"Even if we can't get close enough to kill him," said the other, "at least we can hold him here until the mission is done."

"Ha, you're caught!" it yelled.

Tristan pulled out his knife to cut the net. But as soon as his knife touched it, an array of sparks exploded and the shock caused the knife to fall from his hand."

"Ha! Hey, try that again!" yelled the demon with a laugh.

"Electrified!" said Tristan. I'm stuck. Tristan loaded another arrow, aimed and shot. One of the smaller demons was vaporised with the direct hit of the arrow.

"It's no good," yelled the demon who had triggered the device. "You ain't getting outta here!". Then it turned to one of the others that had joined them. "I'm posting you here, along with some of your other minions. But don't get in the way of his arrows, you morons. He's not going anywhere, but I want to make sure."

"Yesss boss," hissed the demon. "We will keeps him trapped."

"Good!"

With that the larger demons walked off, leaving half a dozen of the enemy on the opposite side of the cavern. One shot off an arrow in retaliation which hit the wall behind Tristan, making them all laugh.

"Great!" said Tristan to himself. "I'm stuck. I can't touch the net, and even if I could free myself, all those demons over there are standing guard, and I have no idea how to get back to that workshop. What about Haans? I can't even protect him. Lord, what do I do?"

8

REMOVED

- mission tristan -

Back in the workshop, Haans continued to carve out the hull of the sailboat. He skilfully guided the chisel along the pencil markings that he had sketched. Originally it had just been a simple block of wood. But with the hollowed out interior, it was now looking very much like a boat that would float in water. He picked up some sandpaper to smooth down the edges. 'This boat will make a young child happy,' he thought with a smile, remembering back to his childhood.

Haans had grown up in a small rural village, just outside of Geneva. He had learnt his woodworking skills from his father who also crafted toys for children during his spare time. Haans had helped his father build their family home which now housed his own children. Coming from a Christian family, Haans had always been aware of the kingdom of God, and had heard the audible voice of God speak to him twice in his life. The first confirmed that Marcellina was the woman he should marry, and they had now been happily married for over thirty years. The second time he heard the audible voice of God, confirmed that he should open up the shop that he was now sitting in.

As he continued to work, an evil presence entered the room. With Tristan caught in a net, deep under the earth, the enemy was freely able to come into the workshop. The bloated potbelly demon shuffled its way across the room. Its short arms and legs protruding from its round body, were unsuited to a battlefield, but it had other abilities with which it could use to influence on behalf of the kingdom of darkness. The six-foot high beast made its way over to where Haans was working. It then plonked itself down heavily across from Haans, on the opposite side of the workbench. It was huffing and puffing with the effort it had taken to walk across the workshop. After taking a deep breath, it slapped both hands on the bench in front of it, and stared pridefully at Haans who was enjoying the project that he was carving. Unaware of the evil beast right in front of him, Haans continued to sand down the sides of the boat.

The demon took another deep breath in and then gave out a loud, long, burp that sent clouds of yellow gas bellowing out into the room around Haans. Haans suddenly started coughing uncontrollably and clutched his chest. Haans dropped to his knees and coughed and coughed, unable to clear his throat and chest. The beast again let out another burp and this time a more dense purple gas came out of its mouth. Haans gasped for oxygen, trying to take another breath, but inhaled the purple gas that was filling the room. Haans fell to the floor doing everything he could just to breathe.

The demon just sat, and a smile developed on its face.

"That's it for you," it said. "You have been removed, and aren't going to bother us anymore." It then tried to pull itself up onto its feet but was unable to do so. "Oh come on, come and get me up!" it bellowed. Just then, two much smaller demons rushed into the room and came around either side of the big one to help it up. "Now, go away!" it yelled at them once it was up on its feet. The potbelly demon turned to walk away, but gave a final glance at Haans struggling to breathe on the floor. "You might survive," it said, "but recovery will be slow." The demon chuckled as it shuffled out of the room.

Haans was still coughing, but now able to at least breathe a little. He picked himself up, still holding his chest, and rested on the bench for a moment or two. He then walked over to the coat rack and pulled his jacket on. "I'm done," he said to himself, as he turned to see the boat that he had been crafting lying on the floor. He went over to pick it up and placed it in one of his large jacket pockets. Haans then went over to the door and took the key off a shelf, ready to lock up. He flipped over the sign on the door which read 'Closed', and then he walked out and locked up. He coughed a few more times as he walked out onto the veranda in front of the shop.

Haans had also started to develop a headache and said to himself, "I'm going to be in bed for a few days after this." He then stepped down onto the pavement, and as he did, tripped and fell, knocking himself out cold.

***

Sometime later, Haans opened his eyes. Everything was blurry. He blinked a few times to clear his vision and looked around. 'Where am I?' he thought. Then he remembered the fall. He put his hand up to his head and felt bandages around it.

Just then a lady came into the room carrying a tray with a jug, cup, and a cloth rested on it. "Oh hello. You've woken up."

"Yes. How long have I been out? And where am I?" asked Haans.

"Almost a day. You are in Doctor Steiner's house, and very fortunate too. We've got eight beds here and this bed only became available yesterday. You'll need to stay with us for a couple more days, just to make sure you are going to be alright."

"A couple more days," repeated Haans, as he settled back into the pillow. Haans was thankful for Doctor Steiner, who had received a large family inheritance and so opened up a part of his house for the sick and elderly. Haans started to think about what had happened.

'The shop is locked up,' he thought to himself, 'so that is good.' Then he remembered the prayer meeting that he was supposed to be going to tomorrow. 'Well, I can't go there now, not in this state. What a shame,' he thought. Haans then closed his eyes and went back to sleep.

9

SPARK

- mission tristan -

3.30am.

David rested his head back on the pillow.

"3.30," he said to himself and closed his eyes. In his dreamy state, he saw a net. He opened his eyes and turned to look at the digital clock again beside his head. 3.33am.

"Prayer time?" he said, still groggy. "Really?"

David rolled out of his bed and on to his knees, resting his forehead on the mattress.

"Better not fight it," he said as he pushed himself up to his feet and went into the wardrobe to pull on his dressing gown. Slowly he walked down the hallway towards the lounge.

"I know, I know," he said to himself. "If I wake up at 3.30am, it means prayer time. I'll give it 15 minutes."

David walked into the lounge and flicked on the lamp in the corner of the room. The soft glow gave enough light to keep him from bumping into anything. He started to pace.

"God, lead my prayer."

Again a net flashed in his mind, and then 'Tristan'.

"Lord, break the net," he prayed as he paced around the lounge. Then suddenly in a moment of absolute clarity, he stopped, drew both hands together, and said, "Break the net over Tristan!"

David stood, hands together, feet a shoulder-width apart, looking straight ahead. The spirit realm shuddered behind David as his prayer-form scrunched time and space. Suddenly a wrinkled white garment was shaken out of the atmosphere. It flapped with the displacement of the connecting worlds. The cloak curved over at the top corners and reached out toward David, wrapping itself over his shoulders. It stretched down his back to create a full length cloak. The top of the cloak extended upwards, fashioning a hood over his head with a gold trim. The cloak rippled in the wind of the spirit and started to glow as did David's eyes. David stood, clothed in the authority of heaven. The spirit realm awaited his command.

"Release!" he declared in a deep, powerful voice. A sudden pulse of light projected off his cloak and expanded to fill the room. Then it immediately imploded into a singularity of brilliant light in front of him. Unable to contain such a concentration of power, the fabric of the atmosphere burst, and the singularity vanished from the realm.

The cloak settled heavily around David as the wind dropped, and then peeled off him in flakes which hung in the air. Then a gentle breeze collected the flakes and blew them through the juncture between worlds. David stood there in his dressing gown. He smiled, still sensing the presence of the Holy Spirit.

"Back to bed?"

Hearing nothing, and having achieved a good prayer time, he now needed to achieve more sleep. 'Have to wake up for work in a few hours,' he thought. So he flicked off the lamp and carefully placed his steps along the memorised path to his bedroom. He peeled off his dressing gown and flopped face down on his pillow. Within a minute he was fast asleep.

***

Tristan was feeling more and more frustrated having spent hours caught in the net. On the other side of the cavern, the demons were constantly talking amongst themselves, sometimes bickering, sometimes sniggering, and sometimes laughing at something that wasn't funny at all.

'They're going to drive me nuts,' Tristan thought. Anxiety and depression began to settle into his mind. He started to believe that he would never escape and that his quest had failed. But then he caught himself. 'The battle is in the mind,' he thought. 'Lord help me to get the mind of Christ. Help me to gain your thinking.' Then a verse flashed through his thoughts. 'For our light and momentary troubles are achieving for us an eternal glory that far outweighs them all.'

He set his mind to gain the Lord's revelation from that verse for his situation. 'The trouble that I'm in, is only light and momentary. That's what your Word says. Not only that, but my troubles are achieving something, they are achieving for me an eternal glory. In the magnitude of that glory, my troubles don't even compare, don't even feature. These troubles are going to achieve for me a glory that will last forever!'

As Tristan meditated on the verse, faith was unlocked within him and he started to feel like anything was possible. His faith became an inter-realm magnet, and it pulled David's prayer from the surface into his realm. Suddenly a spark appeared in the middle of the cavern and hung in the air. The demons stopped chattering and made shushing sounds.

"Look, it's a pretty light," said one.

"It hurts my eyes," said another.

"It's burning my arms," said a third.

The light flickered brighter.

"No, no, no," shrieked the voices.

Suddenly, the spark exploded and filled the room with brilliant light. All the creatures in the cavern raised their arms to shield their eyes from the light, but it didn't matter. They were all vapourised within moments. Tristan also raised his arms to shield himself. A pulse of heat and energy hit him and thrust him back into the rock wall, and the net around him was disintegrated by the power of David's prayer-form.

Immediately all went dark. Tristan blinked as he tried to look around. All he saw was bright spots in his eyes. He rubbed them and looked again. The bright spots slowly cleared and he could see the cavern again.

'I'm free!' he thought. 'But I need to get out of here fast, before any more demons come.' He was reluctant to use the tunnel on the other side of the cavern because that's where the other demons had emerged. Even though he was equipped to fight, he was hoping that he wouldn't have to. Tristan got up from his hiding place and quickly walked around the side of the cavern to find another way out. There didn't appear to be any other exits. Suddenly noises from the other side echoed through the cavern.

"Oh no, back already!" whispered Tristan desperately. The desperation of the situation caused him to look harder with a deeper focus. Out of the corner of his eye, he noticed a dim flash of light. He turned in the direction of the flash and saw a dim streak running the length of the cavern.

"Why didn't I see that before?" he said to himself. "Could it be… a light tunnel! Liberty told me about those."

Suddenly a group of demons burst into the cavern.

"There he is! Over there," said a demon pointing at him. One shot an arrow, but Tristan was ready. Tristan ducked allowing the arrow to narrowly miss him, and made a run for it, dashing toward the light tunnel.

"He's got nowhere to go," mocked a demon. Another arrow was shot at him. Tristan stepped up onto a rock and pushed forward into a dive roll. He landed gracefully on the ground and rolled back to his feet. Stringing two arrows of his own, he released them, taking out both of the demons that had fired on him.

Then he saw a demon break away from the group and rush toward the device that had fired the net.

'Not this time,' thought Tristan as he loaded another arrow. But this arrow was different. Even before he released it he knew that it would form a net. As it sailed through the air, the arrow split apart with a web of light connecting the splinters. The web engulfed the demon, choking it before it got anywhere near the device. Tristan wasn't sure if he had discerned that it was a web-arrow, or whether his faith had transformed it, but he felt that he was becoming more and more in tune with the weapon that God had put in his hands.

"Get him! Get him!" yelled the enemy.

As he ran toward the tunnel, a hail of enemy arrows were shot into the sky and curved over to rain down on him. Again, Tristan prophetically saw in advance what would take place. The answer was still in the arrows. He loaded and fired. As his arrow rose to meet the incoming hail, it exploded sending a shockwave through the air, shattering the enemy arrows, rendering the assault useless. Little bits of wood rained down harmlessly upon him.

With no time to lose, Tristan dived for the tunnel and was immediately caught within the surge of light as he shot out of the cavern at tremendous speed. Being thrust forward head-first, made it difficult to see where he was going. Caverns and caverns hurtled by, then the tunnel curved upward. Within moments he was shot out of the earth and into the sky. All he could think was, 'I just need to get out of here without being killed!' Up ahead the tunnel split off in two directions, with no time to think, he rolled to the right and started to arc downwards towards the ground. Another split was coming up fast. One tunnel disappeared under the ground again, the other ran along the surface. He opted to stay above ground and so rolled left and was propelled along the surface. The tunnel carried him out of the city and into the meadows of the countryside. He rolled again to exit the tunnel.

Tristan skidded along the grassy field. The grass squeaked under his armour as he skimmed along. He let himself slide until gradually coming to a stop. As he lay in the middle of the field, insects buzzed around him, and the sun shone on his face as he lay, looking up at the sky. Tristan realised that he had been holding his breath the whole time. He exhaled, then breathed in deeply. Relieved, he allowed a huge smile to stretch across his face.

"Epic!" he said with a laugh. Shaking his head, he said to himself, "Man, that was awesome. Glad to be out though; I've got some work to do. I need to get to Haans, and find out what those demons have done with him. I also need to give him safe passage to wherever he is supposed to be." He looked to the sky and said, "Help me Lord to find Haans again."

With that he picked himself up. Seeing the edge of town, he began to walk in that direction hoping some kind of marker would point him towards Haans.

10

CROSSING

- MISSION TRISTAN -

As Tristan crested the top of the field he saw a river ahead of him. Across the river was a bridge and beyond the bridge was the city.

He started to walk towards the bridge, then stopped seeing demons standing either side of it.

'How am I going to get past them?' thought Tristan. 'Maybe cross the river further down.'

Tristan took the long way around, out of sight of the demonic posting, and headed down toward the river. He dropped off the grassy verge and onto the sandy stones that lined the bank.

'They'll still see me if I cross anywhere here,' he thought. He brushed the sweat from his brow. 'Maybe I need to cross directly under the bridge, right under their feet.'

Having decided that was the best course of action, he proceeded along the river edge toward the bridge, staying near to the verge.

Every so often he would pass a person or a couple of people

enjoying the sunshine and skimming stones across the water. Then he noticed a boy crouched down beside the water's edge. The boy then straightened up and ran along the edge watching something in the water with a huge smile. Tristan smiled, enjoying watching the boy play. As he got closer his heart nearly stopped. In the water was a little toy boat that looked very similar to the one he had seen in the workshop, way too similar. He walked across for a closer look. When he was nearly beside the boy, the boy let out a yelp and scrambled away. Tristan's eyes grew wide.

"You can see me?" he said.

The boy said, "How many of you are there?"

"What the…?! You've seen others?" asked Tristan.

"No, just Liberty?"

"Liberty? You saw Liberty? How do you know her name?"

"She told me," said the boy who's confidence had now returned. "Are you dumb or something?"

Tristan ignored the boy's comment and asked, "How long ago?"

"Yesterday."

"Okay, anyway, right now I'm more interested in that boat. Where did you get it?"

"Haans gave it to me. He's staying at Doctor Steiner's house at the moment, recovering," said the boy.

"Recovering?!" exclaimed Tristan who was now very concerned that his mission seemed to be falling to pieces.

"You aren't very smart for a spirit," said the boy.

"Look!" said Tristan sternly. "Enough with the smart comments. I'm not a spirit. Well, kind of not. But it is really important that I get to Haans. Can you show me how to get to the doctor's house?"

"Yes, I will help you. I'm Alex," he said, holding out his hand.

Tristan responded, "Well, I'm Tristan," reaching to shake his hand, and went straight through it.

"Haha. That happened last time with Liberty too," said Alex with a big smile.

'This kid is something else!' thought Tristan who also found it amusing.

"So you're comfortable messing with spirits then?" asked Tristan.

"Not really," said the boy, "but I couldn't resist that one."

Tristan let out a sigh. "Shall we go?" he said.

"Sure," Alex responded.

Tristan and Alex continued along the river bank.

"When did you get the boat?" inquired Tristan, pointing at the wet toy boat in his hand.

"Some time ago. Haans has made five now," said the boy, who was looking at the boat, but a look of sadness came across his face.

"What's wrong?" asked Tristan.

"I just hope Haans is going to be alright. He must have hit his head really hard, and his breathing isn't too good either."

"Well, we'll see what we can do when we get there," Tristan answered. "God has us here for a reason, and Haans has a part in saving this city. I have faith that God will heal him and he will get better."

The boy smiled, looking hopeful, "I hope God can do it."

"Of course he can!" said Tristan.

Coming around a bend, Tristan quickly backed into the verge. Alex hustled over to him.

"See those up there?" said Tristan pointing. The boy nodded his head. "It's fine if they see you, but they can't see me, or I'll have a battle on my hands. I need to get under the bridge. Not sure how deep the water is though."

"Oh, it will only be up to your waist," said Alex. "I can walk over and try to distract them if you like."

"Might be a good idea," Tristan responded. "But I don't want you getting in trouble. Why not just walk past them. Hopefully you'll get their attention for a little bit. Just enough time for me to cross."

"Shall do," said the boy who briskly scrambled up the verge and disappeared from sight.

Tristan edged his way along the river, concealing himself under the verge, until he was close to the demons. Then there was a sudden commotion. Tristan couldn't quite see what was going on, but did see one of the demons leave its post and strode off.

'Now's my chance,' he thought and pushed off into the water. Tristan ran through the flowing water under the shadow of the bridge. It was getting deeper and deeper.

'Up to my waist. Yeah right!' thought Tristan, who jumped forward and freestyle swam as fast as he could. Making it to the other side, he turned to see what was going on. He couldn't see what was happening above the bridge. But more importantly, the demons couldn't see him. Tristan carefully climbed the bank on the far side and picked a path through some bushes. He managed to get a good distance away from the river by the time he saw Alex running along the path.

Checking that no enemies were around, Tristan called out, "Alex, over here."

The boy stopped, spotted Tristan and ran over puffing, looking like he'd just escaped from being chased.

"What happened to you?!" exclaimed Tristan.

"I was walking towards the bridge, and the demons weren't taking any notice of me, so I picked up some stones and threw them at one of them."

"You what?!" said Tristan, who couldn't believe what he was hearing.

"It's alright," said the boy. "I didn't let the demons know I could see them. I pretended to be throwing stones in the river. I was throwing them through the demon's head and he was getting annoyed. Then unfortunately one of my stones hit a guy who started yelling at me and came over to give me a hiding. So I ran off over the bridge. I'm a fast runner you know!"

Tristan just stood there in wonder.

"Nice!" he said with a laugh. "Do you get in trouble often?"

"Not really," said the boy. "Maybe once or twice a week."

"That's a lot," said Tristan.

"But that's only when I get caught," continued Alex, "I try to push the boundaries every day if I can."

"Alright, alright. Enough talk. Let's get to the doctor's house."

The two turned and walked toward the city.

Within half an hour they were amongst buildings again.

"His house is this way," said Alex pointing along the road.

Tristan responded, "Now that we are getting to a populated area, you walk on ahead. I'll hang back and try to stay concealed. Let me know if you see any enemy activity."

Alexander nodded, then walked on ahead, keeping a lookout. Just then he noticed shadows moving along a roofline on the opposite side of the road. He looked harder to try and make out what was up there. Unable to do so, he turned to look behind him to see where Tristan was. After a few seconds he spotted him. Not wanting to draw attention to himself by pointing, he wandered back to Tristan to tell him what he saw.

"Up there," he said in a whisper, pointing towards the roof of the building.

Tristan could see the shadows too. "Probably scouts," Tristan said, "on lookout duty… We'll have to be careful."

Tristan did the best that he could keeping out of line of sight, while Alexander continued to walk toward the doctor's house.

Finally they reached the grand three-storied building. It was a beautiful timber house with a row of windows on the ground floor, and another row on the second floor, then two bay-windows protruding from the high thatched roof.

"Great, we're here. Are you able to get in to see Haans?"

"Of course, he's my great-uncle."

"Sorry, I should have asked. I didn't even know that you are related to him."

"That's fine. Follow me."

The two of them entered the double-doors into the house, walked up the stairs to, and into a room with three beds, on one of which was Haans… not looking too good.

"Papa, how are you feeling?" asked the boy.

Coughing a couple of times, Haans turned his head and smiled, "Ahh, Lex, good to see you my boy. I'm doing fine, I just need to keep resting." Alex sat on a stool beside the bed.

Now that he was here, Tristan had no idea what to do next. The assignment had been to defend Haans. Up to this point, Tristan knew that he had not done a very good job. Now that Haans was sick, quite sick. He didn't know what to do next, so he prayed.

"Lord, help."

'Pray for him,' came to mind.

'You mean I should pray for him?' thought Tristan.

'No.'

'No?' responded Tristan.

'Alex should.'

"What? But I don't even think he's a Christian," said Tristan out loud.

"Are you a Christian?" asked Tristan.

"No," responded the boy. "But I do want to go to church. Liberty said I should, and I think I would quite like to."

"You know," said Tristian, "going to church doesn't make you a Christian. Believing that Jesus died on a cross for you, then rose again for you, makes you a Christian. Asking Jesus to take away your sin, and asking him to be Lord of your life makes you a Christian."

"Right," Alex responded.

"Anyway. I felt like God say that you should pray for your great-uncle to get better."

"Me? But I've never prayed before," said Alex.

"Hey, who are you talking to?" asked Haans, still with his eyes closed.

"Can I pray for you to get better?" asked Alex.

"Of course you can. I didn't think you were a Christian, but I'd love you to pray to Jesus for me."

"Ummm, Jesus, I pray you will heal my papa Haans." Alex placed his hand on Haans' shoulder, as he continued to pray. "Make him better, and take away his cough."

"Wow, your hand is really hot," said Haans. "You know, that's a sign that you have a gift of healing."

"It is?" said Alex.

"Yes it is. Keep praying a bit longer," said Haans.

As Alex continued to pray, a glow started to emanate from between his fingers.

"Do you see that?" asked Tristan.

"No," responded the boy.

"There is light coming from your hand. Keep praying."

As he did, beams of light shone all around from between Alex's fingers. His forearm began to glow and veins of light ran up and down his arm. The light intensified to the point where Tristan could no longer look directly at the light and Alex and Hanns were distorted because of the intensity of the rays of light.

The light then began to subside and Alex removed his hand. Haans breathed deeply.

"Well boy," he said, "I'm feeling better already!" Which he probably would have said anyway, but it was the truth. Haans' head was feeling much better and he could breathe.

Then he suddenly remembered. "The prayer meeting is today, I must try to get there," he said.

Haans lay on his bed for a few more moments, then sat up.

"You know Lex, your prayer really worked. I feel great!" he said, smiling at the boy. Alex gave him a hug. Haans glanced over and saw his coat and other clothes in the corner of the room.

"Come on, help me up," he said. Alex put his arm around Hanns' back and helped him off the bed. Once he pulled on his trousers and put his jacket on, he said, "Let's get out of this place."

"Great!" responded Alex with a smile.

The two of them walked out of the room to let the house workers that the bed had now become vacant.

'Impressive!' thought Tristan as he followed them out. 'We are back on again; thanks to Alex's prayer!'

11

ɒOORWAYS

- mission caden -

Caden turned to see the approaching edge of the pavilion. He then disappeared between two of the pillars in a burst of fiery sparks.

Caden looked around in wonder as the sparks faded, and he found himself soaring through glistening clouds of swirling gasses. Sheets of light flashed through them, blending endless colours together. The beautiful array of colour and movement was backdropped by a starry night sky. Up ahead, the sheets narrowed into thin beams of light which traced out a rectangle in front of him. Caden was drawn through the doorway, and pushed out the other side into a wide empty hallway.

Compared to the other-worldliness of his transit, through unknown regions of eternity, this hallway was very plain in comparison. At one end of the hallway were stairs leading down to a lower level, and at the other was a window looking out onto the street below. Caden walked over to inspect the doors leading off into separate rooms. He opened the first door, which led to an empty office. 'No one here,' he thought. Another door had a name on the outside, 'Mr Adam Eriksson'. 'Oh, I wonder if one of these has my assignment's name on it.' He glanced around and saw a metal plaque fixed to a door which read 'Mr. Pierre Gustafsson'. 'That must be the one,' he thought. 'Should I open the door? Perhaps not. Even if he can't see me, he would notice the door opening.' So Caden decided to wait.

Caden pressed his ear against the door and heard a book dropping onto a table and a shuffling of papers. 'Must be him,' Caden thought. 'Better wait it out.' So Caden slid down the wall into a sitting position, with his knees up, on the opposite side of the hallway waiting for Pierre to emerge. Then Caden had a change of mind. 'I'm a bit exposed here if an enemy should come. Maybe I'm best to wait somewhere out of sight. Who knows if there are demons nearby.' Caden decided to go into the empty office that he had first checked out. He pulled up a chair just inside the office with the door open so that he could hear when Pierre came out.

As Caden was waiting, he looked down at his legs and arms. It was the first time that he had the opportunity to check out his armour and equipment. His armour was a pearlescent blue, that emanated its own light in a soft glow. Stardust ran up and down the individual components of the armour. Against his thigh was a sword, and on the other side a knife. On the side of his boots were metal stars. He pulled one off to inspect it.

"Wow, dangerous!" he said, returning it to its place.

It didn't take long, just a few minutes, for Pierre to emerge from the office. Caden heard the door open and so peered around the corner. A middle-aged man emerged, wearing a round-brimmed hat, holding a satchel. His dark green jacket and matching waistcoat were accented by a white shirt with frilly edges, which puffed out of his sleeves and neckline. Wrapping a scarf around his neck, he started walking along the hallway toward the stairs. Just as Caden was about to follow, another figure also stepped through the doorway. Caden quickly tucked his head back into the office, then slowly peered out again. Both had their backs to him, walking toward the stairs. The scaly lizard-like creature with a long tail, was mimicking Pierre's movements. Caden knew he had to follow, so there was nothing else for it. He quickly and quietly stepped out into the hallway and unsheathed his sword. The sound of the metal blade being drawn startled the demon who spun around. Too late. Caden raised his sword, then brought it down on top of the demon. With sharp precision and accuracy, he split it in two. The two halves dissolved into acid on the floor.

With sword still in hand ready for another encounter, Caden followed Pierre down the stairs. The ground floor was much more active. Pierre stepped into the busy foyer. Not wanting to lose him, Caden stepped out too, dodging people as they walked passed. The brick entrance of the building was finely crafted. As Pierre stepped under the archway, Caden looked up and saw spotter demons perched in the corners.

"No! They've seen me!" he said.

Then he heard a raspy voice behind him, "Got you!"

Caden spun around with blade in hand, coming face to face with a warrior demon clothed in chainmail. It made a swipe at Caden with its fist, narrowly missing his face. The prideful warrior had underestimated Caden's abilities. Caden side-stepped, out of the demon's reach. The warrior, loaded with various forms of weaponry, reached for its club with protruding spikes, and swung it at Caden. Caden eluded the blow by flipping into a backward hand-spring. The club came down with tremendous force onto the wooden floor with a crash, splintering the floorboards. Caden then launched his own attack and went for the arm holding the club. He slashed his sword right through the demon's armour, dealing a serious wound to its forearm. The demon roared in pain as black blood ran down its arm.

The warrior dropped the club and unfastened two double sided axes. It ran toward Caden with one in each hand. Caden was in two minds, knowing that his assignment was slipping away, but at the same time, locked in battle with this demon. He reached down to his left boot, pulled off the two metal stars, and flung them at his opponent. As the beast rushed forward, it drew the axe blades in front to act as a shield. Then it backhanded the stars away, deflecting them to the far ends of the room. With both arms raised in the air, Caden saw his opportunity to get close. He rushed forward and slid under the monster, between its legs. Then, rolling back to his feet behind it, he spun around, and slashed his sword down the monster's back. The beast gave a final roar, dropped to its knees, then fell through the ground and disappeared completely out of the realm as if there was no floor at all.

Knowing that time was short, Caden sheathed his sword rushing out of the building to find Pierre. It didn't take long to spot him because there was now a pack of a dozen demons around him. Caden leapt down onto the road to chase them down. Knowing that his presence had already been discovered, there was nothing left but all-out war. Caden reached down for the two remaining stars from the other boot. With one in each hand, flung them towards the demons. Both hit their mark, and two of them fell through the ground like the warrior demon had done. The remaining demons angrily turned their heads looking at Caden.

Caden was gaining ground as he ran, but the demons had many tricks. The tall thin demon at the front snarled at Caden, then reached out its hand and pulled on an invisible door handle in front of Pierre. Suddenly a doorway materialised out of nowhere and Pierre walked right through it. At least a part of him did. Pierre's body continued to walk beyond the door, as if the door was not there at all, while his soul walked through the doorway, and was taken to another place. Pierre's soul split from his body. Half the demons walked through the door as well, with the last quickly closing it. Then the door vanished.

Within a few steps Pierre dropped to his knees and fell face first onto the pavement. Immediately people rushed over to help. Caden was left with the four remaining demons who turned to fight him. One had a crossbow and aimed it at Caden. Caden skilfully deflected the arrow with the armour plate on his forearm, then charged at the creatures. He drew his knife and threw it at the one with the crossbow who was caught up in reloading another arrow. The knife sunk into the demon's chest and the demon dropped through the ground, but the knife remained within the realm and clattered onto the pavement. As the demon disappeared, the crossbow it was holding did not. It also hit the pavement as the knife had done, along with half a dozen arrows which scattered on the ground.

The other three demons drew swords and separated so as to take on the boy from different angles. But it made little difference; Caden had skills. He slashed the first demon's sword out of its hand, then spin kicked the demon in the chest. Then with forward momentum, Caden punched it in the head while it was still off balance. The demon never hit the ground, but fell right through it, disappearing from existence like the others had done. Caden's skill and power was too much for the next creature. He ran forward and dived into a flip with a half twist over the demon. As Caden spun through the air, he slashed his sword through the neck and shoulder of the beast.

The last demon put up more of a fight. Caden defended a blow. The clang of metal on metal rang out across the busy streets, unheard by the people who were walking past, but heard in the spirit realm by demons and angels nearby. Caden deflected another blow, jumped into another spin kick, knocking his foe off balance, then slashing his blade to finish him off.

The immediate vicinity was clear of enemies for now. The only evidence that there had ever been a fight was Caden's knife lying on the ground along with the crossbow and the scattered arrows. Picking up both and collecting the arrows, Caden He sheathed the knife and slung the crossbow over his shoulder. He then turned to find out what had happened to Pierre, and rushed over to the scene. There was the chatter of bystanders and a doctor was checking him out.

"He's breathing fine, but he's unconscious," the doctor said. "Does anyone have water?"

"Yes, over here," said a man holding out a flask and handing it over. The doctor poured some water on a handkerchief and mopped Pierre's brow and face. Suddenly Pierre moved and blinked his eyes.

"Where am I?" he said.

"You seem to have had a fall," responded the doctor.

"I did? Oh well. Please, help me up." Pierre rose to his feet and looked around, seeming a little lost. "I don't know where I am," he said. Then, with a worried expression on his face, he said, "I don't know who I am!"

"You best come with me," said the doctor, "so I can check you out properly."

"Sure," responded Pierre with uncertainty in his voice and brushed down his clothes with his hands. "I should be fine, but yes, you'd better check me out."

"My house is this way," said the doctor, who led him off.

'All I can do for now is follow,' thought Caden. 'What happened to the other part of Pierre?'

12

VAULT

- mission Liberty -

Liberty followed John as he wound his way through the crowded streets. Keeping alert, she scanned the buildings and skies for signs of the enemy.

'Any that were on the ground nearby, must have been destroyed by that massive wave of diamonds,' she thought.

John turned sharply left into a building. Liberty followed him through the entrance. She sidled up to a pillar to avoid being seen by spotters that may be lurking around in the building. John walked to the far side of the large room, filled with people, where there was a man standing behind a desk. She wasn't close enough to hear what they were saying, but the man motioned that John should follow him and walk down the flight of stairs to the left of the desk.

Liberty quickly stepped out from behind the pillar to follow him. Suddenly a hand grabbed her shoulder and pulled her back into an alcove, giving her a huge fright. Liberty spun around to see a familiar face.

"Falcon!" she said. "Don't do that!"

"Sorry. Glad I got to you in time, I was held up."

"You could have said, 'Hey Liberty' or whistled, instead of just grabbing me!" said Liberty, mildly regaining her composure. "You can't just do that to people. I could have run you through with my sword you know?!"

"Are you finished?" asked Falcon.

"Yup," she replied.

Ignoring Liberty's vent and getting straight to the point, Falcon continued, "Down there is the lockup, where the keys are held."

"That's good news," she replied. "Halfway there. First the keys, then the altar."

"Yes," said Falcon. "That's where you are headed, but I can't go with you because the lockup is in the possession of the enemy. I don't know what you will meet down there, but you can be sure that there will be a lot of enemies. You must find the keys to the altar. Have you got the medallion?"

"Oh, yes," said Liberty, feeling her pocket to make sure it was still there. "What do I do with it?"

"It will fit into one of the lockup boxes, where the keys have been safely kept up until now. You will have to rely on the Holy Spirit to lead you because once you are deep in the lockup you will be cut off. We won't be able to see you, and I'm not sure if anyone on the surface will get a prompt to pray while you are down so deep.

"The demons don't know which box the keys are in. If they had the medallion, they would try it in every box until they found the right one. The only reason why they haven't done that yet is because you have it. And let me tell you, it was terribly difficult to get."

"Oh really, where did you get it from?" asked Liberty, who immediately became intrigued.

"It's not so much about where it came from, but how it was made. It took a lot of effort to gather enough people to pray for long enough, to create the medallion. People are quite happy to ask God to bless what they are doing, but they are far less likely to ask God what he is doing, then pray into that. It took a long time to align enough people praying for the unlocking of their city. We got there in the end, and the medallion was created and released. That's the short version of the story anyway.

"Back to you. When you go down those stairs you will see John, but the spiritual vault is far below. You will need to keep going."

Falcon scanned the room. "I've been here long enough. I need to go, and so do you. The enemy already knows you are in the realm and are looking for the keys. Move quickly. Go!"

He gave Liberty a nudge in the direction of the stairway down to the vault. She glanced back as Falcon nodded and turned to leave. Liberty breathed in and let out a short punchy breath, flicked her hair, and quickly headed toward the stairs.

She quickly descended two flights and emerged into a storage facility. John was standing off to the side talking with the man who had led him there.

'I wonder what valuable things John has down here?' she thought. The room looked much like the main floor upstairs, apart from an archway at the far end. It gave her the shivers when she saw it. 'That must be where I'm going - the entrance into the city's spiritual vault. Looks more like a wide open mouth wanting to swallow me up!'

Liberty stopped her thoughts that were trying to cause fear to enter into her mind. 'Faith, not fear,' she said to herself. 'Courage not cowardice'. She crossed the room and descended the stairs through the misty darkness. Cold air rushed up to meet her, stirred by the activity from the lower regions.

For a long time she carefully stepped through blackness, unable to see her boots. She took each step one at a time by feel rather than sight. The air was cold. As she continued to go deeper she noticed a glow below. As she got closer she saw that the light was coming from a flaming torch fixed to the wall. The torch was made of carved rock that looked ancient and beautiful. As she continued down the stairs she passed another and another.

Eventually the stairs opened out into a cavern that was dimly lit by torches around the walls. The cavern was large, full of stalagmites and stalactites, and other rock formations. There were also deep crevasses with bridges over them. There were lots of bridges, going this way and that. She allowed her eye to run through the cavern from where she was to the other side, identifying a path that she could take.

'That looks like it,' she thought. 'But where are all these demons? Everything down here is dead silent.'

All she could do is push forward. Liberty stepped down onto a stone path and proceeded to navigate her way through the rocky formations. Ahead of her was a deep crevasse with a narrow wooden bridge bound with ropes spanning it. She placed her hands on the ropes and stepped on to the bridge. It swayed as she walked, suspended over darkness.

Happy not to be crossing it twice, Liberty stepped off the bridge, back onto solid ground. As she stepped again, she felt a pressure on the front of her boot. 'Tripwire!' Suddenly the silence was broken with the loud rolling of chains echoing around her. She looked up in shock to see a cage plummeting toward her. With no time to move, she crouched and covered her head. 'Bang!' The metal cage hit the ground with exceptional force. Had she tried to jump out of the way and been hit by the cage, she would have immediately been crushed by the strength of the impact.

'They've got me!' she thought.

13

CAPTURED

- mission Liberty -

Liberty's ears were ringing. The echo of the crash still reverberated through the underground caverns. She looked around wide-eyed. She reached out to feel the bars. Hard, solid, cold, and immovable. "Help me Lord!" she prayed fervently. "Get me out of here!"

A flickering light appeared at the far end of the cavern. As it got closer she could see that two figures were coming toward her. 'No!' she thought. Liberty crouched in the corner and drew her sword.

As they got closer, she could hear them talking to each other.

"What's we got this time?" one said. "A trespasser?"

"Yes a nasty trespasser. A trespasser that we can do nasty things to," said the other chuckling.

They drew their swords as they neared the cage. One demon clasped the steel bars with its bony fingers and peered in." Liberty jumped forward and struck her sword against the bars. The demon let out a terrified screech and fell backwards in horror and disbelief. The other peered in as well and the eyes on its ugly face grew wide, and it opened its mouth in amazement.

"It's a girl!" it shouted. "It's a girl! It's a girl! A nasty girl," it said as it jumped around.

'Oh no!' thought Liberty. 'This isn't good.'

"It's a girl!" it said again to the first demon, who had backed away from the cage. "We need to go tell."

The other demon had already started running back to where it had come from. Their voices trailed off into the distance as they disappeared down the tunnel. All was silent again.

Liberty took hold of the bars and pushed with all her might, but it only budged a little. Not enough to give her a hope of escape.

"Come on!" she said angrily. "Someone pray for me!" she shouted, looking up at the cavern roof. She sat back and leaned against the cage, wiping the sweat off her forehead. There was nothing to do but wait.

After some time came noises, a babble of voices from the far end of the cavern. There was chattering, screeching and roaring. A large horde of demons were coming her way. Liberty stood to her feet, ready to defend herself.

A large creature trudged over and stepped up to the edge of the cage. "Hey prisoner!" it said as it thrust a spear through the bars. Liberty slashed her blade in defence, and struck the spear so that it glanced off to one side.

"So, you're the one!" it said. "The one who has come for the keys."

Liberty didn't respond.

"Secure the cage," yelled the demon. Smaller demons surrounded the cage and secured clips on each corner. Liberty hadn't realised, but she had stepped onto a metal plate, which formed the base of the cage.

"Lift!" yelled the demon. Suddenly the sound of chains grating against metal bars high above her echoed around the cavern. Liberty was jolted into the air. Now she felt more vulnerable than ever. She had never been caught by demons before. 'Why don't they just kill me?' she thought.

Liberty was now high in the air looking down on the enemy below. Then the cage jerked sideways, causing it to swing out, and Liberty slid to the other side of the cage. It was hoisted onto metal rails and was pulled toward the edge of the cavern. Ahead of her was a tunnel, just large enough for the cage to pass through. As she entered the light faded and she felt droplets of water fall on her head and shoulders. She eventually emerged from the damp tunnel into a much larger cavern that was well-lit and horrifyingly full of demons. They were pointing and yelling at her.

Looking around the cavern, she noticed little doors all over the walls and the ceiling. 'These must be all the safe boxes,' she thought. 'One of these will hold the key to the altar. But which one?'

"You have something we want!" a shaggy demon yelled from below. It was wearing a crown that had slipped onto an angle, but held in position by horns growing from the top of its head. It held a sceptre in its hand, with necklaces and an embroidered robe tied around its neck. 'Very bad fashion sense,' thought Liberty. The rest of the noise died down. "You will give it to me, or you will fall." Suddenly the cage dropped a couple of feet and gave her such a fright. "Give me the medallion!" it demanded, and the cage fell again.

"Okay, stop!" gasped Liberty. The cage fell again. "Stop, I said stop!"

"You give me it now!" it yelled out.

Then it said "Go!" Two flying demons with hammers flew up to the cage and started banging on two corners. One of the latches came free and the base of the cage opened at one corner. "Give me now!" it screamed. Liberty was flustered. There was no time. What would happen if she fell. Would they kill her anyway? The other demon was still bashing away at the other corner. Liberty reached down to her pocket and pulled out the medallion.

"Here it is," she said.

"Hold it out!"

Liberty slowly reached out her hand. The cage dropped again and she felt the floor about to give way. She stretched out her hand and closed her eyes. The first demon snatched it from her. The second demon stopped bashing the other latch.

Once the demon on the ground had the medallion, it looked up and yelled. "Don't stop, you dumb dumb! She must fall away now. Out of here, girl."

"No!" shouted Liberty as she held to the edge of the cage. The other demon gave a final hard hit and suddenly the floor gave way. Liberty spun around and grasped the bottom of the cage with one hand, leaving her hanging.

"Bye bye, you girl, you go home!"

'Can't be,' thought Liberty. 'Is this mission over?' She looked below into the darkness, then a flash.

"Ha-ha. How long are you going to last hanging there girl?!"

Ignoring the demon, she focussed below and saw another flash. Suddenly she realised, a light tunnel! Like the ones at Riverdale.' This one was not directly below her. If she fell straight down she would fall completely out of the realm and her mission would be over. If she could swing far enough, perhaps she could fall directly over the tunnel and it would take her.

She raised her other arm so that she could hold the base of the cage with two hands. Then she started to swing.

"What you doing you dumb girl? You never swing this far."

"Hey you two," it said. "Go up there and help her fall."

Two demons launched into the air and flapped toward Liberty.

Ignoring the demons, Liberty thought, 'God, I know you saw this before it even happened. It is no coincidence that there is a light tunnel just below me. Even if demons can't see light tunnels, I can and that one's for me.'

The enemy laughed and mocked in the background, but she felt a sense of peace and confidence. Liberty did not allow herself to become distracted and intimidated by the enemy around her. A verse came to mind, 'You set a table before me in the presence of my enemy'. 'Single focus,' she thought. 'Not the enemy, but the mission'.

One of the flying creatures got close, so she kicked it away with her boot. The demons below began laughing, enjoying watching the girl defend herself.

Liberty built up her swing and got a feel for when to let go. 3-2-1, release!

Liberty kicked and flung her body toward the tunnel. The demons watched her fall through the air… then completely disappear…

Suddenly the cavern vanished. Liberty found herself travelling at lightning speed, like her previous light tunnel experience. Flat on her back, arms tight at her sides, she shot through cavern after cavern. At such a speed it was impossible for her to judge what was coming next or where to get out. One moment, she was in darkness shooting through solid rock, next moment another cavern, then straight through rock again. She concentrated and slowed her breathing down to allow her mind to catch up with the exhilarating speed. She knew that if she rolled out at the wrong time, she would either be crushed by rock, or fall into darkness. If either of those happened, she might as well have fallen from the demonic cage and out of the realm.

This tunnel did not turn, but she did feel a slight incline towards the surface. 'I'm getting way too far away,' thought Liberty. 'I need to get out of here soon.' But the tunnel did not break through the surface, it continued to shoot Liberty through the earth. 'I'll leave the entire country at this rate!' she thought. Finally, after minutes of straight high-speed travel, she burst through the surface and found herself hurtling through a rocky landscape at blinding speed. Up ahead was an open space that looked safe to exit. With only a split second to decide, she rolled out of the light tunnel, and was sent hurtling along gravel, creating a huge cloud of dust. Liberty eventually slowed and she squinted her eyes trying to see through the hazy cloud. Then she came to a stop, coughing in the midst of the dirt and dust.

She stood up and brushed herself off, feeling a little dizzy after the experience. Liberty looked around the barren landscape. 'This feels like the middle of nowhere,' she thought. As she spun around in a full rotation to get her bearings, she was confronted by a wall of darkness. The darkness stretched as far as she could see, like a curtain that went on forever. 'Feels like the edge of the realm,' she thought. Then realised in alarm, 'I think this is the edge of the realm!'

Liberty stood half way down a barren, rocky mountainside. 'I need to gain altitude and get to a vantage point,' she thought. 'I've got to get a better look at where I am.' So, she set off with a determination in her stride to get to a better elevation.

After a long hard climb, she crested the hill and saw hill upon hill, as far as she could see. Truly a wasteland, truly the edge of the realm. She just stood there at a loss for what to do. Looking out from her vantage point, she suddenly saw movement amongst the rocks caught her attention. 'No, not more demons!' thought Liberty.

"Over there," one said, pointing at her.

Liberty spun around and ran back the way she had come.

She quickly made her way along a massive split in the terrain, then jumped through the gap between two heavy slabs. Landing on her feet momentarily, but losing her footing, she fell onto her side with a thud. The steep, loose gravel swept her toward the edge of the cliff that fell away far below. Liberty drew her knife and plunged it into the earth and came to a stop as her legs rolled over the edge of the cliff and dangled above the darkness.

Liberty rose, and rushed forward, with the power of a lion within her. She slashed one, then the other, but the third scuttled a safe distance away.

The demon raised its arms and grew to twice the size.

"You failed!" it shouted.

"With the help of God I shall achieve victory for the glory of my God! Now go, in Jesus name!"

With that there was a huge rumbling. The demon in front of her turned to stone, then its shoulder burst, and finally collapsed into pieces and scattered on the ground.

After some time of standing on the mountainside alone, she tilted her head heavenward, "Have I really failed God?"

Silence.

Liberty turned her thoughts toward the Lord, "Should I try and get the keys back?"

No response. "What, you mean I truly have failed?!" she said out loud. A tear of frustration blurred her vision.

Liberty stood at the base of a mountain, on the edge of the realm. She turned to stare out over the edge of the cliff, into darkness, and breathed deeply. Liberty tried desperately to catch the word from the Lord for the moment. 'If I have failed, then why am I still here? Shouldn't I drop out of this realm and be transported back to the surface?'

Just then a thought broke into her mind, 'You will not be able to get the keys back now.'

"What!" she yelled. "I'm not listening to you devil!"

Yet, the voice was peaceful. 'Change of plans,' was the next thought. The Holy Spirit then went silent, allowing her to work it out for herself.

"Change of plans. God of the second chance. God of the turn-around. The one who can turn 'Plan B' back into 'Plan A'." She remembered with a smile that the apparent greatest victory for the devil turned into salvation for the whole world at the cross.

'But if the altar is secured by the demons, there is no stopping them from taking the city. Is there? What if the other two teams gain the atmosphere and the throne as well. Perhaps the enemy will not be able to fulfil its plan. If the red and blue Triaxial Identifiers are secured, is that enough?'

Liberty had just been focussing on her mission, but remembered that she was a part of a larger team. 'What if I completely change my plans, break off from my quest for the altar and pursue either the throne or the atmosphere and help one of the other teams instead? Even if I can't achieve my mission, there's no reason I can't join one of the others. I don't have to be so full of myself to think that I must win my mission if I can help someone else with theirs, but which one?'

Just then there was a thud behind her, higher up the mountain, causing her to spin around. Her eyes grew wide as about fifteen creatures descended towards her.

"What now? Just leave me alone!" she said, as she backed toward the cliff edge. Nowhere to go.

"Do I fight this one? Is anyone praying for me?" she called out.

Liberty backed away from the advancing demons until she could go further. Liberty looked at the drop to nothingness below her. "Help God," she breathed. Liberty looked down at the cliff below her heels, which were overhanging the drop. It wasn't a smooth drop, it was rough but potentially climbable.

Immediately Liberty dropped to her knees, and started to back herself over the edge. She lowered herself down as quickly as she could trying to get as much distance between herself and her attackers. She looked up and saw three heads peer over the edge, as gravel showered the top of her head.

"Keep going little girl," a voice yelled out. "There's nothing down there. We will wait here for you until you come back up. Ha!"

14

UNDERNEATH

- MISSION LIBERTY -

Liberty descended into darkness. As she got lower, she felt the temperature drop rapidly. 'What am I doing, climbing over the edge of the realm into nothingness?!' After some minutes of climbing, she looked up again and saw a head in the distance and faint voices. Liberty wasn't even thinking now, she just continued to climb down and down. Her body was on autopilot. The darkness got thicker, like a fog, making it hard to see the top of the cliff any more. An icy wind started to blow around her. 'I'm climbing out of the realm,' she thought. Countless minutes went by and all was black.

As she continued to climb down, she could make out a red glow beneath her.

'This better not be the fires of hell!' she thought.

Then, after an undetermined amount of time, as she reached her foot down for another foot-hold she found that her foot was hanging over a hazy, red emptiness. The cliff had finished, there was no more realm to climb down. 'The end!' She lifted herself up again so that both feet were resting on rock and she hugged the edge of the realm. Then, breathing hard, she called out, "Help!" There was no echo. The darkness muffled her voice like a wet blanket.

Liberty closed her eyes tightly. Her fingers were stiff. Her toes strained, supporting most of her weight as she hugged the cliff. She felt far away, departed, forgotten, alone. She had been exiled, discarded, cast out of the dwellings of the living. Far from activity, far from life, she hung over oblivion. One soul and eternal emptiness below. Waiting… nothing…

After a time, a thought came to mind, 'You are on the edge.'

"What do I do God, let go?!"

'No!' came the immediate answer. 'Angels don't fly down here and demons hate the empty expanse.'

"So why am I here?" she asked the voice in her mind.

'To walk,' came the response.

"Walk where?" she asked again.

'Walk under.'

'Oh,' she thought. 'I'm going quite nuts. My imagination is telling me I can walk through nothingness'

'You can walk under the realm!' came the strong thought. 'Reach down to the edge and look underneath.'

"No, I will fall!" Liberty exclaimed

'Trust me.'

Liberty reached down with her right hand and felt the underside of the realm. As she did something very strange happened. Her reality shifted, gravity shifted. She found that she had such a good grip with her right hand, that she lowered her boot to hook it under the edge, then the other, finally she released her left hand and reached over to take another handhold under the realm. She pulled her body under until she found herself climbing up and over the bottom of the ledge. Liberty rolled over to a crouching position, then very cautiously stood up straight.

"What! I'm standing under the realm?!… Or in a new one?" she exclaimed.

All around, a soft red light hung over the landscape. As she looked up, or rather down, whatever your point of reference was, she saw a giant red sun hanging in the sky. She instinctively knew it was very old.

The ancient dying star had lit this realm eons before the earth realm had ever existed. Its heat had since dissipated, and the outer layers of the star had been expelled into space forming the beginnings of a nebula. The dull steady light did not flicker, and had lost all ability to sustain life.

The dim light gently illuminated her surroundings.

The rocky surface was generally flat in every direction, with silhouettes of aged shapes and structures periodically interrupting the landscape. The structures looked like molten lava had erupted, then immediately turned to stone, forming fluid shapes, that had then fractured and broken in ages past.

The rocks were sprinkled with quartz, causing little red sparkles of reflected light dusting the surface.

She stood in one of the first realms ever created, long forgotten. Once a centre of activity of movement and life, now only the shell was left; the bones of an existence, lost in the memory of a forgotten sun.

Though Liberty had emerged from above, she did not feel upside down at all. The gentle gravitational forces on her body held her to the base of the realm. The forces were not as strong as normal, which made her feel much lighter. She was so light in fact, that her hair floated around her, rather than naturally falling toward the ground.

'Walk,' said the Holy Spirit in her mind.

'Wow, I can walk under the realm and get to the other side, or any side. But isn't that going to take a long time?'

As she walked she felt that she was covering large distances with ease. 'Am I really walking the length of the entire realm? Why not run?' Liberty picked up her pace. Her strides were long, and each landing was a gentle touch.

As Liberty ran, her mind wandered, 'I am far away from the surface, from my earth home, and at the same time I am far away from the spirit realm too. I am in a place where angels don't fly and demons fear to tread. How many souls have even been to these parts? Am I the first and only, or have there been others? Probably questions that will never be answered.'

Her long strides felt good in the light gravity. She felt graceful and that she could continue to run all day and all night, if that was even a thing down here.

Liberty was enjoying running through a more or less weightless environment. With each stride she pushed forward, propelling herself over great distances. She built a rhythm as she picked out good launching points for each step. Caught up in the flow of her movements she hadn't noticed that more nothingness was getting nearer. As she looked up, Liberty realised that she was coming to the end of the rocky surface, so she slowed down. Her hair floated in front of her, so she pulled it back to keep it out of the way.

"Am I here?" she asked no one in particular.

She stepped forward with the toes of her boots hanging just over the edge. She looked down and saw the cliff face rising way above her. Again she found herself on the border of two realities. She most certainly felt that she was standing on the top of a realm, with a red sky above her, but below was the long climb upwards toward sunny Geneva.

Liberty reached down over the edge, finding good handholds. She lowered her leg identifying a secure hollow in the rock to dig her heel into, then gripping hard she let her other leg go to swing around and dangle over the edge. She reached up, finding a crack to wedge her fingers into. She couldn't really describe the feeling, but gravity shifted around her, and she found herself on a cliff-face with nothing below her and an entire realm above. Her hair was most definitely falling toward her feet now. 'I wonder what would happen if I let go?' she thought. 'Best not try,' came to mind. 'Good idea,' she responded. Liberty started to climb.

After some climbing, leaving the red glow behind, Liberty was breathing hard so decided to have a rest. Tilting her head upward, she puffed some loose hair away from her face.

'How much further? What does it matter? I just have to keep going.' With that, she reached higher to the next hold and her hand grasped something that felt like a branch. 'Seems secure,' she thought. As she pulled up, she realised that it was a little tree growing out of the side of the rock, no larger than a foot high.

'Oh, a single little tree. That's lonely,' she thought as she looked around out into the darkness. She looked back at the tree again and noticed some white flower buds. 'Well, you are unexpected.'

Using it to pull herself up, she rested her knee on it, and reached higher.

***

Lucy, a young five year old girl from Liberty's church, was playing with toys in her room. Her stuffed toys were all lined up on her bedroom floor, including Boris the bear, a white and black snow tiger, and all her Minions. She was holding her unicorn in one hand and a stuffed hippo in the other.

"I will get you!" she shouted, as the unicorn jumped high and landed on the hippo, knocking it to the ground. "You are no match for me!" Just then a picture of a flower came to mind. "Flower! You grow," she said. Then she turned her mind back to the epic battle that was raging across her bedroom floor. The unicorn flew through the air to finish off the hippo who was no match for the unicorn's power and agility.

As she prayed her child-like prayer, sparkles burst out from around her. They splayed out in all directions, then rose up to meet at a point above her head. Together they formed the shape of a bud encompassing her. The sparkles continued to rise, twisting around each other like a rope extending high up into the sky, and then sent to where they needed to go.

Lucy had partnered with God through a simple prayer to achieve his purposes. Even though she had little understanding of what she was doing, she had made herself available to be used by God.

***

Little sparkles exploded around the buds and half a dozen of them opened into white flowers. The tree also grew slightly and her boot got snagged on a branch. As she wrestled her boot off the branch, the roots started to dislodge.

"Wow you've blossomed!" she said in awe as she lowered herself back down to take a closer look at the flowers.

Then she remembered reading Psalm 1 and said, "I can't leave you behind. I'm going to plant you beside a stream." She reached down and it came away surprisingly easily in her hand. It had held securely to aid her climb, but when she decided to uproot it, it came away freely. Liberty undid the strap that held her sheath, pressed the small tree against it, and re-strapped it tightly to her thigh.

"Hope you last. You should be okay there for a while," she reassured.

Liberty continued to climb and eventually crested the top of the cliff and she found herself on the east side of the city.

'Now I have a decision to make. Do I head toward the Elemental Stone and help claim the atmosphere, or do I make my way to the throne to claim authority over the city? The Elemental Stone will be closer to where I am. So it makes sense to go and try to find the stone.'

Just then an angel landed beside her.

"Falcon!" she exclaimed.

"I lost you," said Falcon. "Where did you go?"

"Did you know that you can walk under this realm?" said Liberty with a smile.

"Yes, I've heard that it's possible, but I don't know of anyone who has ever done it. And now I do," said Falcon. "We don't know everything. There are many assignments that God initiates that I don't understand. There are even realms that no angel or demon or any other created thing will ever go to, apart from God who created them all. In fact there are infinite places. So you have now been somewhere that I will probably never go. I have assignments of my own that I must carry out in distant places and you will have yours."

Falcon finished, though Liberty could tell that he could say more, much more. But she felt not to press him for more information, even though she loved hearing him talk about eternity. There were probably many things that he was forbidden to say.

"So what now?" asked Liberty, who felt again the pain of failure. "I failed," she said.

"It is true that by now the enemy probably has the keys to the altar and they will use them against the city as soon as the red and blue axes are aligned. The altar is the last piece to put in place, so they won't use the keys against it until then."

"I was thinking that perhaps I could help one of the other teams fulfil their quest."

"That won't do any good," replied Falcon. "If the others succeed in their missions, the red and blue axes will cross the altar, giving the enemy the opportunity to insert the keys. It all depends on who has control over the altar. All the demons have to do is switch the keys, placing the left key in the right slot and the right key in the left slot. Then, instead of the life-giving golden light of the altar's axis, darkness will rise over the altar and the city. The city will then be lost for perhaps centuries, or forever."

Liberty immediately felt awful having failed, having let down her friends, and effectively handing over the city to her enemy. She had failed everyone including God.

"Can I steal the keys back before the other teams fulfil their quests. Is that my next move?"

"I don't know," responded Falcon. "In some ways it seems

impossible to regain the keys now. But we must look for an answer and look for one soon. All has been set in motion. The meeting between John, William and the council is in just one day. The other two teams are aligning their axes. We must do something to win the altar."

"What's this you have there?" said Falcon, noticing the plant strapped to Liberty's thigh.

"Oh, I found it on the edge of the realm. It looked like it didn't belong, so I wanted to replant it. It seemed the right thing to do because it helped me climb up the cliff."

"You are right that it doesn't belong. The last time I saw one of those was millenniums ago, before the flood. It's a Dydadem Tree, one of God's special trees that was in the garden from the beginning. But it was not allowed to continue to grow because of its special properties."

"What properties?"

"It's flowers change the state of things, causing them to take on another form. It never makes the same change twice. It is one of the artiflowers that were prohibited to continue growing on earth after sin entered the world. Its leaves are also powerful for bringing healing and restoration."

"Can I use it to help my mission?"

"I don't know. Keep it with you. Let's go. We need to get back into the city."

15

EXCHANGE

- MISSION CADEN/LIBERTY -

Suddenly Caden heard a familiar voice behind him, "Caden!".

Caden spun around to see Jack approaching him.

"Jack!" said Caden relieved, "So glad you are here. Good to see you again!"

"Good to see you," Jack responded. "Sorry, I've been held up and I've got here too late. The enemy has Pierre."

"Well the enemy has a part of him at least. I saw Pierre get split, and half of him disappeared, then his body dropped to the ground. What part of him was taken?" Caden inquired.

"His memory," Jack responded.

"Oh, so not his soul then?"

"If they had his soul, he'd be dead," said Jack dryly.

"I guess so."

"If you lose your soul, it's like losing your head, you are quite dead. It's like no Wi-Fi, no data, and a flat battery. It's like…"

"I get it, I get it," interrupted Caden, who knew Jack was playing with him. "So they have his memory then. What does the enemy want with his memory?"

"The enemy doesn't want his memory at all," responded Jack. "They just want to separate it from him, so that he forgets where he needs to be tomorrow."

"So we have to get his memory back?"

"Yes we do. We need to somehow reunite his memory with the rest of him, but I'm not sure how to do that," responded Jack. "We can at least track down Pierre's memory and hopefully an answer will present itself as we go. There's no point staying with his physical body at this stage. The enemy could attack it with sickness, which wouldn't be good, but the most important thing now is his memory. We need to open our own door and follow."

"You can do that?" asked Caden.

"I'm an angel aren't I?" responded Jack.

With that Jack reached his arm out, and drew it out to the side. As he did a sliver of light broadened and a doorway to another realm opened. They both stepped through and closed the door.

***

The landscape was rocky and barren. Caden looked up. Stars sprinkled the skies above. The stars looked close, popping off the inky blackness surrounding them.

Jack and Caden looked up the sloping terrain and saw the squad of demons walking away with Pierre's memory in chains. Just as they were about to follow the group, they heard some shouts.

They turned to see Liberty and Falcon walking towards them over the crest of a rocky outcrop.

"Hey Caden!" shouted Liberty waving at him. Caden rushed over and gave her a hug.

"Amazing seeing you guys here," said Caden.

"Ha! I didn't expect to see any of the rest of the team on my own quest," said Liberty.

"Neither," responded Caden. "If only our quest was going better."

"Oh, are you having trouble?" asked Liberty.

"You could say that. My assignment's memory has been split from his body and is held captive by a squad of demons. We somehow need to reunite his memory with his body, so that he can remember to make the important meeting that he needs to be at tomorrow."

"I've got problems of my own," Liberty replied. "The enemy has the medallion and probably the keys to the altar by now. So I've practically failed my mission."

Falcon greeted Jack, "Hello Jack"

"Falcon, good to see you," Jack responded.

"Much is against us. Our options are limited, and time is running out," said Falcon.

"Yes, we need to make the most of what we have, and plan our next move," Jack replied.

Liberty and Caden continued to talk, catching up on each other's adventures, while Jack and Falcon conversed between themselves.

"What?!" exclaimed Jack. "A Dydadem tree, where?"

Falcon motioned across toward Liberty who still had it strapped to her thigh.

"I've never seen one," said Jack. "But we could use it now. Its leaves could help to restore Pierre's memory to his body."

"True!" responded Falcon. "She was supposed to find it. It is in her possession for a purpose."

"What about the altar?" Jack said.

"I'm working on that," responded Falcon. "First let's get some of those leaves so that you can continue with your mission."

"Hey, you two", called Jack, as the two angels walked over. "We have a plan. At least half a plan."

"Excellent," said Liberty with raised eyebrows. "Half a plan?!"

"Suppose it's better than quarter of a plan," said Caden.

"Those Dydadem leaves can be used to restore Pierre's memory," said Jack.

"Oh of course," said Liberty. "Falcon, you told me that the leaves can restore things."

"That's right," responded Falcon. "If we can take some of these leaves and get Pierre's memory to eat them, his memory should be drawn back to his body again."

"So shall I pick some?" inquired Caden.

"Just take one for a start and see what happens. The tree may need to be replanted before they work."

Liberty unstrapped the plant, then Caden reached out and plucked a leaf. He held it up and it glistened in the light. But then, after a few seconds, it withered in his hand.

"Oh no," said Caden. "Look it's shrivelled up!"

"Yes," responded Falcon. "I thought it may have to be planted. Try a flower."

Caden plucked off a flower and held it up. It too glistened, but also moved as if a gentle breeze was blowing between the petals.

Falcon said, "The flowers have life within them. They will last for perhaps a day once they are picked. If the tree is planted beside a life stream, a leaf will also last for a few hours."

"Do the leaves know if the tree is planted?" inquired Liberty

"Kind of," responded Falcon. "It is the life stream that remains connected. When the tree is planted and draws the water from the life stream into its leaves, the leaves and the tree will be connected for a time, even once the leaves are picked. The stream is what makes the connection. But the leaves will only hold the water for a few hours and then the bond will weaken, until the leaves shrivel and their properties die.

"Right," said Caden. "So we need to plant the tree next to a stream, take some leaves, and then make Pierre's memory eat them. Is that the plan?"

"Yes, I'm hoping that will work. But as for the altar and Liberty's quest, we will take some flowers which will at least give us options. I'm not yet sure how they will help restore the altar, but we have a day to work it out, provided we are not already too late."

Caden handed the flower to Liberty so that she could get a good look at it. As she cupped it in her hand, each of the five pearlescent petals swayed back and forth. The petals created a funnel in the centre, which was encrusted with small diamonds. The diamonds refracted the light causing mini rainbows within the flower.

"It's beautiful!" exclaimed Liberty.

"We need to get moving," said Jack. "Sounds like we have a plan, or at least a partial plan. Caden and I will take the tree. Falcon and Liberty, take as many flowers as you need. I'm sure the Lord will reveal a purpose for them."

Falcon handed Liberty a sash. She took it and delicately plucked another four flowers, and placed all five in the sash. She then slung it over her shoulder.

"We are going to head over in this direction," said Falcon, pointing between two large rocks off in the distance.

"The Lord be with you," responded Jack. "We'll head over that way," he said pointing in the direction that the enemy had taken Pierre's memory. "There also happens to be a life stream over that way too. If we hurry, we can plant the tree and then catch up to the demons."

"Great, I'm ready," responded Caden.

They parted company. Jack and Caden moved off quickly, while Falcon and Liberty took a different route, in the direction that Falcon had pointed out.

"What's over this way, apart from the city?" asked Liberty, pointing ahead of them.

"There's a junction point, a place where light tunnels intersect. I'm not sure what we are going to do yet, but at least from there we have options for travel."

Then Falcon said, "Thirsty?"

"What?" said Liberty, thinking that it was a random question. But perhaps not so random, because she was very thirsty and knew that Falcon was always looking out for her best interests.

"There's a stream over there too. Not a life stream, but you can get a drink of water."

"Sounds good, I need one," she responded with a smile.

16

OUTPOST

- MISSION CADEN -

The two had been running for quite some time.

"How are you?" Jack called, as he turned behind to see Caden following at a distance.

"I'm good, I've found my rhythm, this is a good pace," he said.

The pair of lonely figures tracked through the barren landscape in pursuit of the demon horde. Light from a bright star cast two long shadows down the slope, as they jogged along the ridgeline.

"No light tunnels in these parts," Jack called out. "And the enemy knows it. They will be taking his memory to one of their holding chambers, up one of the Dawn Pillars I suppose. You can just make them out, off in the distance," Jack said pointing.

Caden could make out some needle-like silhouettes protruding from the earth.

Jack slackened his pace a little so that Caden could catch up and they could run together.

"They are called the Dawn Pillars because they have stood since the beginning, and a life-stream runs between them. Originally they were a sign of hope, before the enemy took control of them and turned them into prisons. The river still runs between them. There's nothing that the enemy can do about stopping the flow of the river, but they will attack anyone who tries to get close. So get ready for some engagement," said Jack with a wink.

"This is one of the most remote life rivers. It flows in from the edge of the realm and sweeps in between the pillars, then curves back out into the distant wastelands. Provided we can keep enough distance between us and the lookouts, we will hopefully be able to get to the river unnoticed. Then we can plant the tree out of sight somewhere along the riverbank. After that we will need to get to the pillars themselves. There are three. The enemy has holding cells at the top of each. Hopefully we can work out which to climb."

"Oh, we will be climbing?" asked Caden.

"Yes, we will need to. The demons have claimed them and have set up access points at the bases for themselves so that they can get up and down them easily. We can't use their transport tubes, just like they can't use our light tunnels. So we will have to climb up the outside one of the pillars."

'It should be Tristan doing this, not me,' thought Caden. 'He would be far better.'

'This is for you to do,' came the response in his mind. Caden felt comforted that the Holy Spirit was speaking and with him in the middle of his quest. He thought back to climbing Razor Peak with Tristan, and the other climbs he had done with Tristan since. 'I can do this,' he thought.

The enormous pillars were taking shape as the two got closer. Sweat had developed across Caden's brow, and he wiped it with his forearm, and kept moving.

After what felt like hours, Jack slowed down to a walk alongside Caden.

"We will have to be aware now and keep careful watch. There will be spotters. They may be on alert because they have a prisoner, but I don't expect they know we are coming, and it is very unlikely they know we have a Dydadem Tree."

They pushed on, carefully looking out for any slightest movement amongst the shadows.

"Shall we track behind that ridgeline?" said Caden, pointing to a set of jagged hills over to the left. "It will take us longer, but might mean less chance of being seen."

"Yes, I was just thinking that. Good plan. Let's pick up the pace again, and get that tree planted. Are you good to go?"

"Yes, let's do it," responded Caden, as they broke into a jog again, slightly changing course, heading to the left of the ridgeline.

As they dropped down into a valley, Jack looked up noticing movement. He raised his arm and created a fist, indicating that they should stop.

"I saw movement up there," whispered Jack.

Caden wiped the sweat off his brow again and the two of them gazed up at the spot for a minute or two.

"There! See that?" whispered Caden.

"Yes, I saw it. It's an outpost. Now we have a decision to make. Do we risk continuing along our path behind the outpost, hoping they don't look down here. Or do we go up and attack, hoping that none escape to raise an alarm?" said Jack.

"Either way it's dicey," responded Caden.

"I think we need to eliminate the outpost," said Jack. "Not only do we need to plant the tree upriver, we also need to get to the pillars unseen."

"Nothing else for it," said Caden. "We need to get up there and take them with the element of surprise."

Jack and Caden began to traverse up the slope, using the shadows amongst the rocks to conceal their presence. They plotted their course from large rock to large rock, keeping out of view as much as possible. As they got closer to the outpost they heard grumbling, and the muffled sounds of a number of demons having an argument."

The two crouched behind a large slate slab to take a breather.

"We're close. You ready to fight?" asked Jack.

"Ready as I'll ever be," Caden responded.

Suddenly an arrow pinged off the rock just in front of them.

"We've been spotted!" said Jack, who spun around in the direction the arrow came from. A silhouette of a demon with a crossbow could be seen lying on a rock behind them. They had passed close to where the demon was perched, and had obviously missed each other. Now the sniper had the two in its scope."

"Hit the outpost now!" said Jack with urgency. "And watch your back. We'll take the sniper afterwards."

Jack and Caden rushed from their position toward the outpost.

As they ran up the slope another arrow flew overhead and hit a hanging metal gong in the outpost. The warning sound resounded through the air. Demons rose in alarm clambering over themselves to find their weapons. Jack and Caden were still a distance from the camp, giving the demons a chance to weaponise themselves. The demons stood at the ready to take on the intruders. Jack and Caden were outnumbered, four to one, with a sniper behind them. The odds were not good.

***

Benjamin reached high to grasp the next handhold. Getting a secure grip, he raised a leg and pushed his toe into the notch in the rock. Gradually, hold by hold, he scaled up the rock wall overlooking Riverdale. He hoisted himself up onto a ledge to take a breather. As he looked out over the vista of Riverdale, his friend Caden came to mind.

'Be awesome to have him up here with me,' he thought. Then he decided to pray for Caden.

"Heavenly Father, I pray for success and health for Caden today." Then the story of Jonathan and his armour-bearer came to mind, and how they defeated the Philistine outpost and gained a victory for Israel.

"I declare victory in Jesus' name!" he prayed.

In the spirit realm there was a loud 'snap' that echoed around the cliffs.

After a couple of deep breaths, Benjamin turned to face the rock wall again. He reached behind his back and dipped his fingers in his chalk bag. He then placed a hand on the next hold to begin the next section of his ascent.

***

As the two rushed closer, there was suddenly a loud snapping sound, followed by the ground beginning to shake. Rocks split around them with loud claps of noise. The demons were thrown off their feet, giving Caden and Jack the chance to get closer and engage their enemy. Caden was just about to strike the closest demon with his sword, but before he could, the demon split and shattered like the rocks that were crumbling around him. He looked in surprise as the remaining demons suffered the same fate, one after another.

"Duck!" yelled Jack, and Caden dropped flat to the ground as another arrow whistled past from the sniper.

"Over there!" Jack yelled, pointing ahead.

Caden looked and saw what he was pointing at. He quickly got up and rushed over to pick up a crossbow that was resting against the wall. It was already loaded with an enemy arrow. He spun around with the weapon ready to fire at the sniper. He lined up using the scope and pulled the trigger. The arrow whistled out of the bow, sailed through the air, and directly hit his target. The demon slumped, then rolled off the rock it was lying on.

"Great shot!" said Jack "That one was obviously out of range of the prayer-form."

"Prayer-form?" inquired Caden.

"Yes, someone was praying for us, or rather you. That is what gave us the victory this time."

"Do you know who it was?" asked Caden.

"Do you?" responded Jack with a smile.

"No idea," said Caden.

"You'll have to ask around when you get back," he responded. "Let's not waste any more time. We need to get down to that river, plant the tree, then figure out how we are going to get to the prisoner."

With that, they both rushed down the slope, back on course for the river.

17

PLANTED

- mission caden -

After much navigating around rocks and boulders, Caden and Jack made it to the river bank huffing and puffing.

"There's a good spot over there," Jack said, motioning with his hand. They made their way over to where the river had produced an inlet, surrounded by large boulders. "We're out of sight here, let's plant the tree."

Caden stepped into the water, just ankle deep.

"How about right here, in the middle of the inlet?" said Caden.

"Yeah," said Jack. "That'll work."

Caden got down on his knees in the water, and began to shift stones and hollow out the silt. Once it was deep enough, Caden unstrapped the tree from his thigh and set it in the middle of the hollow that he had made. Immediately the tree responded and its leaves straightened out. Caden then covered the roots with earth so that it was secure. He then washed his hands in the water and stepped back.

As the two watched it, it began to sparkle.

"It's growing, it's actually getting bigger as we watch," said Caden.

"Wow look at that," Jack said pointing to one of the branches that was reaching out with new life. This branch looked different from the rest. As it grew it curled up at one end. In fact, the branch looked crafted, rather than grown.

"It doesn't have leaves on that one," Caden said.

Jack considered this for a while, then walked over to the tree which was now nearly as tall as him. He reached through the leaves to take hold of the branch that was different from the rest. As he took hold of it, it easily came off in his hand. Jack drew his arm back and walked over to Caden.

"What is it?" inquired Caden.

"I don't know. It's not long enough to be a staff and it doesn't look like a weapon. I don't know what it is for, but I do know that we are supposed to have it."

Jack placed it in his pack.

Caden reached out to pick some leaves. The leaves came off easily in his hands as if the tree was giving them to him. The leaves remained strong and full of life in his hand.

He placed them in his sash and stepped out of the water.

"Let's go," said Jack. "We have what we need to continue with our mission."

As they walked away down river, Caden glanced back to have a final look at the tree. It continued to sparkle, with sparks falling into the water causing the inlet to glow. Small rainbows refracted onto the surrounding rocks.

'Such a magnificent tree,' he thought. 'It looks out of place, hidden away like this. It should be planted in the courtyard of a grand palace.'

Then he prayed, "Don't let the enemy find it."

As they came around a bend in the river, the two of them looked up to see the pillars looming overhead.

"This is as far as we can go walking in the shallows without being seen," said Jack. "We are going to need to cover the rest of the distance by swimming."

Boulders scattered periodically within the river, with rapids encircling them. The undulating surface should conceal two heads, especially if no one was expecting to have intruders.

"So we float down-river then?" asked Caden.

"Yes, that's what I'm thinking," said Jack. "But we still have to choose which pillar to climb. Fortunately the river flows between all three."

"That far one looks like it has the most activity around it," said Caden. "See how demons are going in and out of the cave at the bottom. The closer two just have demons outside, and far less activity."

"Agreed," said Jack. "We will need to float past the first two, then get out at the last one. Probably best to float beyond all the pillars, then we can circle around to the shadow side. We should be able to climb it from the far side unnoticed."

The two waded into the water. The current was stronger than they had expected. The water felt good, washing away the sweat and dust of their journey so far. Caden lowered himself into the rapids and felt the water seep into his armour. He was tensing his legs, trying to hold himself in place until his whole body was submerged. Then he lifted his legs and immediately the water swept him down-river. Caden stretched out his arms and paddled a bit to help him float, while keeping his head as low in the water as possible so that he wouldn't be seen from the shore. Jack was doing the same, keeping a careful watch to make sure no enemies were looking in their direction.

The pillars looked much taller up close. The three pillars looked enormous, silhouetted against the starry sky.

As Caden raised his head to maintain an awareness of his surroundings he noticed a large dragon-like creature take off from the base of one of the pillars. Its huge wings pushed downwards, lifting it off the ground. Clouds rose into the air, as it stirred up the dust. Flapping to keep its heavy body airborne, the dragon flew toward the river.

'Not good,' thought Caden. 'They can't see us from the shore, but from the sky we are much more likely to be noticed.' Caden quickly glanced across the surface of the river to find an appropriate rock to hide against. Coming up was a large rock to his left. There was nothing he could do but swim across the current, hoping that raising his arms out of the water wouldn't be noticed. He made a sprint for it.

Jack could see the situation and did the same. They both made it to the rock and hugged it tight, with the current pushing against them.

"Do you think it saw us?" asked Caden.

"We'll soon find out," said Jack. "Are you good to hang on for a bit?"

"Yes, I can hold on," responded Caden.

"Down!" said Jack urgently, and they both submerged themselves, still holding on to the rock, while the large shadow glided past.

Caden stayed down for as long as he could, then burst up through the surface, gasping for air. The creature was still flying overhead, swooping low, then rising again.

The creature circled back towards them.

"I hope it doesn't keep this up for two long. We can't stay here forever. But if we are seen, we will have no chance of getting to the pillar," said Jack.

The creature flew low over their rock, and then alighted on another rock down river. As they watched, it settled very carefully, so as not to get wet. As its tail lowered, the tip of it touched the water, and it immediately pulled it up, yelping as it did. It then curled its tail around its body so as not to touch the water again.

"Doesn't like water," said Caden. "So why is it sitting in the middle of the river?"

"They might be setting up extra postings. Knowing that time is short, they want to be extra careful," responded Jack.

"Well, there's no way we can get past that dragon without it seeing us," said Caden.

"I know. We're stuck now," Jack responded.

They waited hoping that the dragon would move. They could see its evil eyes looking out over the waters, scanning for intruders. As it did, every so often it would change its position on the rock, scrambling and clawing at it, trying to maintain its balance. Sometimes it looked like it was staring straight at them, but then it looked away again. As time was being lost, and claw-marks on the rock were being gained, the two were feeling more and more anxious.

Then the beast repositioned to look at the pillars. This was the first time that the dragon had settled to look in the opposite direction, with its back toward them.

"Quick," said Jack urgently. "Go for its tail!" and he let go. Caden was taken by surprise, but let go as well. He placed his full trust in

Jack's plan, whatever it was. The river swept them quickly toward the beast, and suddenly they were there. Jack kicked his feet out against the rock and allowed the current to push him up and he immediately grabbed the dragon's tail, wrapping both arms around it, and pulled it out over the water. Caden hit the rock, jumped up, and landed on the outstretched tail, and also grabbed it tight and pulled down into the water using all of his effort. The beast let out a scream and plunged into the water behind them.

Caden immediately saw the water around him blackening, and the tail in his arms began to get slippery and dissolve. Looking back he saw a wing rise out of the water, but the rest of the body was immersed in the river. Within moments the beast was gone and the two continued to drift in the middle of an inky blackness that had surrounded them.

'Yuck,' thought Caden.

The waters cleared, and at the mercy of the current, they floated amongst the pillars. Above the rushing and gurgling sounds of the waters, they could make out the faint shouts of demons yelling, and perhaps even laughing.

They drifted past the first two pillars and then passed by the shadow of the third. They allowed themselves to drift further downstream, out of the range of lookouts. As they floated from between the pillars, into a flatter landscape leaving the pillars and enemy behind them, Caden started to paddle his arms and swim towards the river's edge. His boots touched the riverbed. Staying low he walked through the water, finding a suitable place to leave the river, behind a rock. Jack followed.

As the water dripped off their armour, Caden combed his hair back with his fingers and brushed the drips off his face and arms.

"You good?" asked Caden.

"Yes, good," Jack responded. "Sorry, I couldn't explain. I just saw the opportunity and took it."

"Well it worked!" Caden smiled. "I guess it was unwillingly posted, and we were able to take advantage of the fact that it hated water."

"That's right. But we need to keep moving. We should stay out of sight if we take a direct path from here to the pillar."

"It's looking clear to me," said Caden. "Are you ready to make a break for it?"

"Yes, let's go," said Jack.

18

PILLARS

- mission caden -

They rushed from behind the rock and made a dash for it as quickly as they could. Caden was the first to reach the pillar and threw his body against it. Moments later, Jack did the same. They took a rest, then made their way around the base to the far side of the pillar. This side was shrouded in shadow and faced out across the vast wasteland toward the edge of the realm. The enemy had not set up lookouts on that side, because no one would ever approach from the direction of the wastelands, or so they thought.

"You set for a climb?" asked Jack.

Caden again recalled the climbs he had done with Tristan and responded, "Absolutely! It's high, but has a rugged profile, so there should be plenty of holds. We will have to pace ourselves though and hopefully find some good ledges to rest on."

They began. The initial incline was easy enough to get up on all fours. No real climbing for that first section. They then reached the vertical face. Caden found a crack in the rock, offering a good climbing line with holds all the way up to the next section. Hand over hand they gained elevation. Every so often Caden shook out his arms relieving the lactic acid build up. He pulled himself up onto a ledge and Jack came up after him.

Now a long way above the ground, they both looked out over the wasteland backdropped by the starry night.

"Careful there. Some loose rock," Caden said, kicking some gravel off the ledge.

"All good," Jack responded. "You can see the edge of the realm from here."

"What's beyond it?" asked Caden.

"Nothing much," Jack responded. "Just space and all the stars that you can see. Beyond those stars are other realms. They go on pretty much endlessly."

"Wow, are there whole races and ways of life in the other realms?"

"Well, I don't know everything. But I do know that all the realms are full of created things and endless design. But in most of those realms there are no souls, nor will there ever be. The realm that you are from is the one that the Father loves, the one that Jesus died for. Out of all the vastness of all the realms and ages of the heavens, there is one singular sphere, the earth, that is the centre of God's focus. God has not spread his love equally, he is totally invested in his plan of salvation for his people on earth."

"It's amazing to think that God places such a high importance on people."

"You are created in his image, and it is his will that not one person is lost. Everything he does, he does for people."

Caden continued to look out, and think about the vastness of God.

"Let's press on," said Jack.

Climbing was harder from that point with more stops and breathers required to manage energy levels. For hours and hours they climbed until the end was in sight. They were so far up that the river looked like a thin blue ribbon.

"We're almost there," Jack whispered. "I don't know if we will encounter demons at the top, or if Pierre's memory will be there by himself. Either way, we need to prepare ourselves.

Caden was the first to carefully place his fingers over the top. What he felt was surprising. It felt like a flat, polished surface. He eased his head up so that he could peer over the edge. Immediately he saw Pierre's memory sitting in chains. The golden outline of the man glowed. The shape looked like Pierre, but without a solid body, his memory could have been mistaken for an angel or some other kind of created being. Surrounding the flat tabletop surface were six pillars marking out the corners of a hexagon. Caden looked up, and to his horror, noticed a vulture-like creature perched on top of one of the pillars. As he quickly glanced around he then saw one on each of the six pillars. He quickly withdrew down to meet Jack.

"Bad news," said Caden. "There are demons that look like vultures on pillars that are surrounding the top. It is a prison without walls, and guarded by those creatures."

"How many of them?" asked Jack.

"Six I think."

"We need a plan," said Jack. "We need to get Pierre's memory to eat some of those leaves, then need to work out how we are going to escape."

"Can you open up a door for us, the same way we got into this realm?" enquired Caden.

"Unfortunately not. Not here where the enemy has control. I can only open doors in neutral locations. We will have to think of something else."

"What if we don't need to escape?" said Caden. "What if we just get these leaves to Pierre. Maybe that is enough for us to complete our mission. It doesn't matter what happens to us after that."

"It's risky," Jack responded. "I feel like there is still more for us to do. I think we need to try and escape."

Just then, there was a screech that sent shivers down Caden's spine as one of the vultures dropped off its perch and swooped down looking angrily towards the intruders.

"Quickly up!" said Jack.

They both hoisted themselves up onto the surface at the top of the pillar. Four of the creatures had jumped off their perches and swooped out into the air, ready to attack the invaders of their territory.

"You get over to Pierre," shouted Jack, "and I'll try and hold them off."

Caden unstrapped the crossbow that he had picked up at the outpost, and threw it over to Jack. It had arrows mounted to the side of it. Caden then rushed over to Pierre who looked up in surprise at Caden.

"We've come to help. Quick, eat these," Caden said hurriedly. He pulled out two leaves and handed them to Pierre. Pierre had a concerned expression, not knowing if he should trust this person he had never met. Suddenly the worried expression turned into an evil one and he attacked Caden, forcing him to the floor. Pierre jumped on him, chains and all. He tried to scratch at Caden's face. Caden kept Pierre at arm's length and tried to squeeze his leg under Pierre's body to kick him off. Caden then noticed a small dart in the side of its neck, and realised that he must be under demonic control. Caden then used all of his strength to raise his leg and kicked him off. He immediately rolled onto Pierre, pinning him to the ground with his forearm pressed on Pierre's chest. Then, with the leaves in his hand, he forced them into Pierre's mouth. A sudden change took place and the anger left his face. Caden yanked out the dart from Pierre's neck and threw it off the side of the pillar. Pierre looked stunned as if he had just woken up from a bad dream.

"Eat and swallow!" Caden said. As Pierre swallowed a wave of peace came over him and he started to fade into mist. As he faded, he looked directly at Caden and smiled. Within a few seconds, he was gone.

Caden leapt up with sword in hand, and ran toward Jack. Jack had already shot down one demon. They stood back to back in a two-man fighting formation, defending each other. Jack fired again and hit his next target. A vulture swooped toward Caden, but Caden lunged forward, slicing his sword through the air, cutting off its head. The body fell to the floor with a thud and Caden kicked it off the edge.

"Three left," said Jack.

"I've got a plan," Caden replied. "See if you can shoot down one more. We need to grab the other two."

"Grab?!" asked Jack surprised.

"Yes, and force some leaves down their throats!"

Jack thought about it for a second or two, then responded,

"Brilliant!"

Jack shot again and knocked another demon out of the sky. Caden passed a couple of leaves to Jack. The two remaining demons swooped out over the expanse in opposite directions, and turned inwards to make a unified attack.

"I'll take the one closest to me," shouted Caden.

As the demons came within close range, both Caden and Jack dropped their weapons. Caden stepped to the side, then thrust his arm forward and grabbed the neck of the vulture. Both Jack and Caden were thrown backward. Caden felt winded, but managed to hold on. Surprised, by the hand-to-hand combat strategy, the demons squawked. Caden then lifted his legs and wrapped them around its neck and pulled its beak back. He then quickly threw a couple of leaves down its throat and held shut its beak. Immediately the bird went limp. Jack had managed to roll over so that he was on top of his vulture, and he too forced the leaves into its mouth. Then there was silence on the top of the pillar. The birds were held down long enough for them to swallow and then were released.

"What now?" asked Caden.

"Ready to fly?" responded Jack with a smile. "The leaves have cut off the evil intent of the demons for a time, and have also given them extra strength and vitality. They can fly us off this rock."

"Excellent!" Caden responded.

"Get up!" Jack commanded the demons.

The two demons got to their feet and stood side by side, looking at their new masters.

Both Jack and Caden went over and sat on the edge of the platform, with their legs hanging over the edge. Caden looked down and chuckled, enjoying being so high up. The two birds flapped over and reached down their claws. Caden reached up to take hold of the legs of the creature, while the creature in turn grasped Caden's forearms. Securely locked in, Caden slid off the edge of the ledge, placing his entire trust in the creature and the effect of the leaves.

Caden stomach lurched as the creature plummeted toward the ground under the weight of its passenger. The vulture flapped furiously, straining its wings to gain some kind of control. It transitioned into a glide for a rapid descent. Being so high up, both vultures were able to glide over the river and over a number of ridges before getting close to the ground.

As they skimmed a ridge, Jack yelled, "Release!" Both Jack and Caden were dropped and landed on their feet, skidding down a gentle slope. They broke into a roll to ease some momentum as they descended down the slope. As they came to a stop, Caden raised his hand, and Jack slapped him a high five.

"Off you go, into the wastelands," said Jack to the birds, who gladly took off, being released from their heavy loads.

"The effect of the leaves will keep them from returning to the enemy for a few hours," said Jack.

"We did it!" said Caden with a big smile. "We freed Pierre's memory."

"Yes we did. We best get back to him and see how he is. We still need to keep a careful watch over him."

"Can you open a door here?" asked Caden.

Jack nodded and drew his arm across his body, took hold of a spiritual door handle and pulled it open. A shaft of light opened up. Caden stepped through and so did Jack. Then he closed the door behind them.

All that remained on the silent shadowy slope was the impact of their landing, and footsteps that led to nowhere.

19

REUNITED

- mission boys -

The golden mist gathered. It swirled around itself hanging in the empty expanse, halfway between nowhere and somewhere else. It gently moved, rolling in on itself, as if it was alive, but without direction or form. Winds blew from various directions, shaping the cloud, causing it to form the image of a man. The edges became clear and glowed with light. Then it suddenly fell backwards, and dropped an endless distance. Waterfalls of light cascaded down around it. Falling, falling, then whack! It hit his body.

Pierre suddenly sat up in bed, startled, and said, "I remember!"

He rubbed his eyes, wiping away a sleepy tear rolling down his cheek.

Just he heard his name being called.

"Pierre!"

Pierre turned his head toward the door to see who it was. The familiar face of his friend was peering in.

"Haans!" Pierre said. "What are you doing here? And what happened to you?" looking at the bandage around his head.

"Oh, I just had a fall. I'm fine though," responded Haans. "What about you?"

"I really don't know. I suddenly fainted and woke up with amnesia. Couldn't remember a darn thing!" Pierre continued, "but I'll tell you what I do remember, I've got a meeting to get to in Choulex. So I need to get out of here."

"Oh, you're going as well? The prayer meeting?" responded Haans.

Pierre laughed, "Yeah. We can go together. I already organised a stagecoach a couple of days ago."

"Oh great, I haven't been in a stagecoach for a while," said Haans, as he helped Pierre out of his bed, found his clothes, and got him ready to leave.

****

Suddenly, a sliver of light opened up in the corner of the room. Startled, Tristan unsheathed his sword. Two figures stepped through the light and into the room. Tristan gripped his sword tight, ready to fight the two figures that had infringed on his space. As the brightness faded, the details of their familiar features could be seen.

"Caden! Jack!" said Tristan in surprise.

"Tristan?" said Caden. "Ha! Awesome to see you," as he stepped over to give him a hug. "How's it been going so far?"

"Bro, it's been mental," responded Tristan. "We can catch up on the story later."

"Hello," said a young voice.

"Well, what do we have here?" said Jack, smiling at the boy.

"I'm Alex."

"I know," said Jack.

"You do?" said the boy, surprised.

"Yes. I'm an angel and you have been given a special assignment," said Jack walking over to him and crouching down to Alexander's level.

"I have?" said the boy in wonder.

"Yes. I now know what this is for," Jack said, lowering his pack and removing the object that had grown from the Dydadem tree. "I'm going to give this to you and you need to deliver it to someone for me. Are you able to do that for me?"

The boy nodded excitedly as he took the wooden object in his hand.

After further instruction Jack raised himself to a standing position. Haans and Pierre looked set to leave.

"Alex," said Haans. "You, alright? What are you doing talking to yourself?

"I better go," said Alex excitedly. "See you later." With that, he walked out of the room waving and acting like he was holding something in his hand.

"Sometimes that boy is away with the fairies," chuckled Haans.

Pierre gathered his belongings, and they both headed towards the main doors of the house.

"Seems like we are back on track again," said Jack to Caden and Tristan. "Let's go." The three of them followed the two men out of the house. They all walked towards St. Peter's Cathedral in the centre of town, where the stagecoach was waiting for them.

***

The three followed Haans and Pierre at a distance, keeping a watchful eye for enemies who might be out and about. As they neared the centre of town, demonic activity increased and so they hung back watching from the safety of an alleyway.

"We aren't going to be able to follow them through town," said Jack. "I think the best idea is to catch a light tunnel to the edge of the city and wait for the stagecoach to catch up. Hopefully nothing happens to them between now and then."

"How far is the closest one?" asked Caden.

"Just down the road. Follow me," Jack responded.

The three stole down the road, remaining concealed from scouts on the rooftops and demons on the ground. They ran amongst the buildings and crowds of people.

Unfortunately, a dark figure soared high above them, with bat wings, and eagle eyes. It was so high that it was only a distant spec to anyone looking up into the sky from the ground, but very little escaped its telescopic vision. The high altitude scout saw the humans, and tracked their movements as they quickly hustled along the roads.

"It's just up ahead," said Jack.

The boys couldn't see it initially, but as they drew nearer, the faint tunnel became more obvious. They came up alongside the tunnel and Jack looked along its length to see where it headed.

"I'll go first, but you will need to jump in almost immediately to remain close behind," said Jack. "Stay sharp and follow my lead. I can't remember if it is the first or second left that we need to take. I'll also need to work out our best 'drop point' on the fly." Then Jack smiled. "By the way, it's fast!"

"I know," said Tristan. "One of those has already got me out of trouble."

"Great!" said Jack. "Caden, your turn to experience angel travel."

"Let's do this!" he said.

The three lined up, one behind each other, with Jack in front.

"Ready? Go!" said Jack.

All three jumped sideways into the tunnel and were immediately thrust onto their backs, and shot forward at extreme speed. The first split shot past almost immediately. Suddenly Jack pulled left, so did Caden, then Tristan immediately after him. The boys were wide-eyed, and concentrated hard so as not to lose their guide. The tunnel rose slightly into the sky, then Jack pulled hard left again. They boys did the same, and banked around toward the ground in a large curve. Suddenly Jack disappeared which took Caden by surprise. So he rolled out of the tunnel a split second after Jack had done. Tristan was last to roll out lagging by about a second.

Jack landed gracefully on his feet, skidding down a grassy hill, dropping off the verge and onto the path. Caden emerged with arms spread wide, balancing himself as he flew through the air, landing on his feet momentarily, then was engulfed by a bush. Tristan appeared on the far side of the path, landing perfectly on his feet, using his momentum to spin around and launch into a backward flip, clearing a rock, and back to his feet again. He spun around with a big smile on his face to look at where the other two had ended up. Seeing only Jack, he looked around worrying where his friend was. Then he saw movement from a bush and Caden clambered out. He was splitting leaves out of his mouth, and wiping himself down. Tristan burst out laughing and fell to the ground, holding his stomach. He kept laughing until tears ran down his cheeks. It was light relief from the intensity of their mission so far.

Jack, initially feeling bad that he had led Caden into a far from optimal landing, started to laugh too, seeing that Caden also had a smile on his face.

"Oh, what a shocker!" Caden shouted with a chuckle, still wiping himself down. "I got hit by a bush!"

"Dude," said Tristan sitting up. "That bush wasn't moving!"

"Ha-ha," Caden responded "A second later and I would have made a perfect landing."

"Nah, don't think so," said Tristan, enjoying the moment at his friend's expense.

Caden just smiled, feeling no need to respond.

"Oh well," said Jack. "At least we are still in one piece and are roughly where we need to be."

The three walked back along the path, toward the city looking for a good spot to wait out of sight. The sun was bright and felt warm on their faces. Bugs buzzed around them amongst the long grass.

"Look, that must be it," said Tristan, pointing as the stagecoach crested a hill.

"Great! At least we can see them now. Let's wait under that tree until they get here," said Jack.

As the stagecoach approached, Jack said, "You will need to try and stay as hidden as possible. When the coach passes, I'll jump onto the roof so as to divert any attention of the enemy onto me instead of you, and you can sit on the ledge at the rear of the coach."

The coach rumbled along the path, and as it passed under the tree that the boys were hiding behind, they leapt out and pulled themselves onto the ledge on the back of the coach. Caden and Tristan then lowered themselves to sit on it with their legs dangling down.

"You good?" came a voice from above. They looked up to see Jack peering over the edge of the roof. Caden gave Jack the thumbs up.

They travelled along for quite some time. As Caden and Tristan talked with each other, Jack kept a lookout. Dragon-like creatures circled the skies over the city, but the enemy didn't monitor much of what was happening out in the country.

The coach continued across fields and passed through the tree-line and into the woods. As they rumbled along, shafts of light broke through gaps in the leaves of the trees.

"Keep a lookout," Jack called down. "We don't have as much visibility here."

Caden could hear Pierre and Haans talking in the coach as they continued their journey. After some time Jack called down from above, "It feels to me like we aren't heading in the right direction, like we have veered off the path somehow."

"Oh, really," Tristan responded. "What should we do?" No response. "Jack, you there?" Tristan called again. Still no response, Tristan looked at Caden. So Caden tried.

"Hey Jack!"

Then came the sound of a familiar voice.

"We're all good," came the response.

"Where did you go Jack?" Tristan called.

"Just went scouting for a moment. We're all good," he said.

"Right," responded Caden, sounding unconvinced. "We're all good then."

"We're all good."

"Maybe I'm just a bit jumpy," said Tristan to Caden, "thinking we'd lost Jack."

"Yeah, weird," said Caden.

The stagecoach continued to navigate its way along the path through the trees. As it did, Caden and Tristan noticed thin cone-like rocks protruding from the ground, scattered amongst the trees. The further they went, the more cones there were, and less trees. The landscape was changing. The boys then felt the coach begin to descend slowly. All greenery faded, and in its place, bare rock dominated the landscape.

"Hey Jack," Caden called. "What are all of these rocky things?"

"We're all good," came the response.

Caden whispered to Tristan, "We're not all good."

"I know," Tristan responded. "I'll see if I can take a peek over the roof."

Tristan got to his feet, reached his fingers over the roof, and pulled himself up so that he could peer over the edge. He gasped then lowered himself back down again.

"Jack's gone," Tristan whispered. "There's a demon up there."

"We need to get off," responded Caden. Tristan nodded. Quietly the two eased themselves down and dropped onto the path. Quickly they rushed off the path and crouched down behind a rocky outcrop.

20

PATHWAY

- mission boys -

As the coach slowly moved away, for the first time, Caden was able to see for himself who, or what, was on the roof. A cloaked demon had the reins and control of the stagecoach.

The boys watched the stagecoach rumbling its way down the path, going further and further into the distance.

"We need to move now," said Caden urgently, "while we only have one demon to deal with and not a thousand!"

"I'm ready. Time to fight!" responded Tristan.

Tristan unslung his bow. "Let's get as close as we can. I'll take out the demon on top, and you get up there and see if we can pull the coach around."

"You're on!" said Caden as they pounded fists together.

The boys leapt up from their hiding place and started to run along the path. By now there was a great deal of distance between them and the coach, but they made up ground quickly. Just then the demon on the roof turned to look at them. Its expression was a mixture of surprise and fear, which then turned into determination as it flicked the reins, pushing the horse to pick up its pace.

Before the gap could widen again Tristan stopped momentarily. He quickly drew an arrow, loaded it, and pulled the string back to his cheek. He exhaled and released, shooting the arrow with deadly accuracy, piercing beast's armour between the shoulder blades. The demon slumped forward and toppled off the coach. Caden sprinted as fast as he could to catch the runaway coach. He reached for the back of the coach and missed. He ran on further, stretched out his arm again and caught it.

Caden pulled himself onto the ledge and reached up to the roof to hoist himself up. Taking a few steps along the roof, then dropping down to the front, he grasped the slack reigns and pulled back. The horse responded immediately and came to a halt.

"To your left!" yelled Caden from the roof. Tristan looked across and saw an enemy speedily floating over the rocks towards the stagecoach. The demon looked like an octopus draped in a moth-eaten cloth. It was fast. Tristan loaded another arrow, drew back the string, tracking his arm with the demon's movement. Seeing a clear shot in between the rock, he released the string and the arrow sailed clean through the cloth. Tristan thought he had missed, so reached for another arrow. But within moments, the demon fell toward the ground and disappeared from sight.

Desperately, Caden was pulling on the reins trying to get the horse to turn around but there wasn't much room. The horse neighed and finally came around, pulling the stagecoach behind it.

Back on the path again, Caden flicked the reins to push the horse forward, and off it went. The horse was obviously far happier going back to where it had come from, rather than towards its doom in the demonic stronghold. As it trundled passed, Tristan leapt up onto the stagecoach and climbed onto the roof to join Caden. There was no point trying to conceal their presence now.

As they raced back along the pathway, more rag-covered demons appeared from between the rocks, gliding toward them with terrifying speed. Tristan shot off more arrows, striking down the enemy one by one. But it was only buying them time, rather than giving them the upper hand. For every one that Tristan took down two or three replaced it.

"We're getting more and more company," said Tristan, as he shot another. The demon slapped the ground and tumbled with flaps of rag reaching out, trying to hold itself within the realm. But it rolled into oblivion, disappearing from sight. Three cloaked demons had now made it on to the path behind them and were gaining ground quickly. Tristan waited for his next shot. As one demon glided behind another, he shot, knocking both to the ground at once. As they fell, another two joined the path in pursuit.

"We shoot one down, then it's immediately replaced by others!" shouted Tristan.

"I know!" Caden shouted back.

Just then Caden looked down, and right beside him was a cloaked demon, reaching out its bony hand toward Caden. Caden immediately reached for his sword and drew it out. While holding the reins in one hand, and the sword in the other, he slashed the demon's arm off. It let out a screech and veered away.

"I want to fight, not steer!" shouted Caden

"You may get your chance!" Tristan shouted back. "Tree up ahead!"

The boys had made good distance, back into more tree-covered territory where the demonic influences were less pronounced, but now a tree blocked the path.

The stagecoach pulled up in front of the tree which had obviously been cut down since passing that way. Both boys, with drawn swords, jumped off the coach, ready to protect their passengers. The enemy glided in from all directions.

Caden raised his sword and rushed forward. Grasping the handle with both hands, he swung his blade, slicing through his enemy, then carrying on the momentum of the swing, he spun to slash through another. Then, in a moment of clarity and focus, Caden felt at one with his weapon and the world seemed to slow down. He could feel the muscles in his body and each finger curled around the hilt of the sword. He saw a pathway forward from one demon to the next. He rushed at them, knowing their weaknesses. God was helping him. With startling speed, Caden cut through the enemy to his left and to his right.

On the other side, Tristan had the same experience. He felt faith rise in his heart, and knew the weaknesses of the enemy. Tristan ran and jumped over fallen logs and rocks, skilfully wielding his blade through the air, dropping more and more demons. He felt the perspiration build up around his body as he continued to cut through the onslaught of wave after wave. Tristan decided to move back, closer to the stagecoach again so as not to get too far away from his assignment.

"Caden," Tristan shouted.

"Yeah," Caden shouted back, still battling the enemy.

"Seems endless. Wave after wave," Tristan shouted again.

"I know," said Caden. "Need back up."

Just then a thin sliver of light appeared beside the path. It opened up and Jack stepped through.

"Hey, where have you been?!" yelled Caden, a little annoyed, but also relieved at the same time.

"Long story," he responded. The serious expression on his face indicated that it had indeed been a long story.

"I've got one of these," he said, drawing out a sphere from his sash.

"Is that a prayer-orb?" called Tristan.

"Yeah, you know about these?" Jack seemed surprised.

"Layla told me about them from our last mission," said Tristan. "Got the hammer?"

Jack reached into the sash with his other hand and drew out a small silver hammer. He then ran over to the coach and jumped up onto the roof for maximum impact.

"Close your eyes!" he shouted, and brought the hammer hard down onto the orb. With a sudden flash of flame and explosion of energy, the orb exploded, lighting up most of the forest.

Fire fell from the sky and blazed around them in a sweeping circle. As the stream of fire hit the ground the flames spread outwards consuming the enemy.

The ragged demons all darted away in an attempt to outrun the fire, but they were not fast enough. The flames continued to rain down in ever widening circles, setting every creature on fire. The fire did not harm the grass or the trees. Not a leaf was singed, but the enemy was engulfed.

As the light slowly faded, the boys lowered their arms from shielding their eyes. Blinking and looking around, they saw no more sign of the enemy, and even the tree that had blocked their path had been blown out of the way.

"Let's go," said Jack, as he dropped down on to the front seat to pick up the reins again. The boys jumped up on to the coach.

"You might as well sit up here now," said Jack. "You're known, but hopefully we can make it in time, before the enemy recovers and provides reinforcements."

The stagecoach set off again through the forest, but this time on the correct path for Choulex.

"So where did you get to?" asked Caden.

Jack let out a sigh, then said with raised eyebrows, "Doorways!"

"Doorways?" responded Caden. "Did you get pulled into one?"

"Yep. Opened up right in front of me. The enemy must have been tracking us and known our exact location. I was pulled in, then had a fight on my hands. I was detained for a while, but was able to escape and go to get extra help. The Spirit had prompted your uncle Andrew to pray. It was a good prayer, as you can see," he said, with a wink.

"Ha," said Caden. "That was uncle Andrew's prayer-orb? I'll have to ask him to pray for me a bit more regularly when we get back."

***

Indeed Uncle Andrew had prayed. Having returned from work he sat in the car on the driveway for a moment or two, listening to the pouring rain coming down on the roof.

"Better make a dash for it," he said. "It's not going to ease off in the next few minutes."

Just as he was about to open the car door, Caden came to mind.

'A good lad, that boy,' he thought.

'Pray for him,' came the next thought.

'But I need to get inside,' arguing with his second thought.

'Fine, when you get inside then,' came the response.

With that he grabbed his laptop bag and quickly opened the car door, jumped out and slammed it shut. Running toward the front door, he fiddled with his keys trying to find the right one. The front porch covering gave some relief from the rain and enabled him to unlock the front door without getting any more wet. Once inside, he hung his coat up and switched on the jug.

'Right, better pray then,' he thought, walking into the lounge.

"Lord, I lift up Caden to you…"

As Uncle Andrew prayed, metal plates started to form around him. Once fully formed, they slammed into his body covering his arm and legs with armour plating. Every time a piece of armour hit his body, he felt the anointing of the Holy Spirit urging him to pray more.

As he continued to pray in the middle of the lounge, with more pieces materialising and being fitted to his body, another object began to form just beside where he was standing. As Uncle Andrew pushed back the work of the enemy through prayer and declared the blessing of God, a huge dragon-like head formed, nearly half Uncle Andrew's height. Uncle Andrew raised his right arm and Leviathan shot across and locked on to his arm, becoming one with his prayer-form. Standing like a mighty, armour-clad warrior, with the head of an awesome beast as a powerful weapon, he stretched his arm out straight up. As he did, the dragon's mouth opened and a burst of flame shot into the sky. The raging stream of fire intensified as Uncle Andrew moved his arm back and forth.

Demons within the neighbourhood hid in any shadowy place they could find, trying to escape from the heat and intense light.

As Uncle Andrew said, "Your will be done!" a final burst of fire blazed into the sky. High above the house, an orb formed, which collected the flames as they raged into it. Andrew then lowered his arm and thanked the Lord for his presence. The large head slowly dissolved and the pieces of armour unlocked from his body and drifted away through the air. Andrew could of course not see any of this, but did feel the tangible presence of the Lord.

As he walked back into the kitchen, he flicked the jug on again because it had already boiled and flicked off the switch a few minutes earlier, which often happened. Sometimes it would take two or three flicks before he actually poured a cup of tea because there always was something to do around the house. With friends coming for dinner soon, he opened the fridge and started to get the vegetables out to make his favourite Turkish kebabs.

***

Having experienced the flames of Uncle Andrew's prayer, the stagecoach was now freely trundling its way through the forest at speed. Jack was back at the reins again with the boys on either side, staying alert for any more ghostly creatures.

21

time

- mission liberty -

Liberty drank from the river and splashed water on her face, while Falcon sat looking up at the stars… thinking.

Liberty's thoughts turned towards her friends, so she decided to pray for each of them. Picturing Samantha's face, she put up a special prayer. The story of Samson came to mind and so she said, "Give Samantha strength." As soon as the words were out of her mouth, a ribbon of angel-light wound around her arms, then burst in a flash and disappeared.

'Wow,' she thought, 'She must have needed that. I hope someone is praying for me too.'

Liberty paced around in circles while she was praying, kicking a stone along the dirt which then pinged off a rock. She kicked another stone into the stream making a 'plop'. Liberty turned her thoughts back to the waters, and how she got to Geneva in the first place, being carried by the time river. Then an idea started to formulate in her mind. She spoke her thoughts out loud.

She turned to Falcon and exclaimed excitedly, "How did we get here? We went back in time right? Can we go back in time and try again? Give us another chance at completing the mission. Can we do that?"

Falcon responded, "You can't go back to a place you have already been, because your spirit can't be twice in the same place. You can only have a single point of existence for your spirit in the earth realm. The earth realm is bound by time which brings limitations on time-shifting."

"Then how come you are here?" Haven't you existed throughout all of earth's time, since before creation? You must have been here before, so why aren't there two of you? Is it different for angels?"

"It's quite different for angels. We can't step back in time at all because we have always existed throughout earth's history. At any point on earth's timeline we are already there, which prohibits us from time-shifting at all."

"But you came back with me for this mission didn't you?" asked Liberty, trying to understand how Falcon could be here too.

"Oh no, I've never met you before. I didn't come back in time with you at all. This is my time, where I live at the moment. You have come from the future entered my time."

"You are kidding!" said Liberty. "But what about Riverdale? What about the battles we've engaged in together? What about all that we did on our previous quest?" Liberty suddenly felt an empty space inside. There was a piece of her life, shared with a friend, an angel, someone who knew her that hadn't happened yet, at least for one of them. Now it seemed that Falcon didn't know her at all. They had never spent those moments together yet. Falcon could see the sadness and disappointment on Liberty's face.

"Don't worry Liberty. I do know you. All the angels know the people they are assigned to. You are known in heaven before you live your life on earth. We wait for years, centuries, to finally meet those whom we will help. Right now is our first meeting for me, but in the future it will be our first meeting for you. The history you have with me is real because it is yours. In a few hundred years it will be mine too. It is a privilege for me to work with you in two different times."

"It's just weird that you haven't helped me save Riverdale yet. It's like this is our first mission, and Riverdale is the sequel," said Liberty, who was trying to get her mind around the ramifications of time-shifting.

"Did I do okay?" asked Falcon with a playful twinkle in his eye.

"You were amazing!" said Liberty with a smile. "But you couldn't have done it without me," she said grinning.

"Oh I'm sure you displayed all the faith, courage and skill to get the job done. I'm only here to help, to aid you in the mission."

"So what happens anyway," asked Liberty, "if someone goes to a time they have already been? Does the universe explode or something?" said Liberty trying to think of time-travel movies.

"Ha – no. If you go down the time river and try to jump out where you already exist, you just slide past that point until you can enter where you haven't been before. It is like two magnets with the same charge; you can't push them together, the force between them keeps them apart and they slide past each other. It's like you can't go left and right at the same time, you end up going one way or the other. Or just stand still of course, but you have to eventually move sometime," said Falcon.

"What about getting back to my normal time?" Liberty asked.

"There are two time rivers. One river flows back through the passages of time, and the other flows forward. You can jump into the forward time river, up to the point you left, and that is where the forward time river ends. You cannot go any more forward than the place you originally left, the river stops at that point and empties you out just after the same time you left. No time will have passed. The river that flows backwards continues flowing to the beginning of time. But like I said, we as angels have never travelled these rivers."

"So let me get this straight. Only humans can time travel, and not angels or demons?"

"That is correct. Humans exist on earth for just a short time, which gives a lot of scope to freely move about through the vastness of earth history. We can't move backward in time at all because all angels and demons have existed all of earth history up until this point. We can't go to where we have already been.

"These rivers continue to rush through earth time, but are hardly ever used because everything is basically achieved in its own time. God can always achieve his purposes with the people who live in the local time. But every so often he assigns someone to time-shift."

"How many humans have time-shifted?" Liberty asked.

"Including you?" responded Falcon.

"Uhhh, yeah," said Liberty, guessing that she wasn't going to believe the answer.

"Ha, I'm not going to say just one. There's been a few, though not many because it's not usually needed. Each mission has its purpose. As you know in your own Christian journey, the path is never straight or straight forward. All sorts of unexpected things happen. The main thing though is to have faith."

"Anyway," said Liberty. "This mission requires us to go back in time in the first place, just to be here. Is there a chance that I could go back further in time to prevent the demons from taking the keys?"

"You can't change the past. You can't change the fact that the demons already have the keys," said Falcon.

"Well, can I go back earlier and change the keys?" asked Liberty.

Falcon stopped to ponder what Liberty had just said. Then reasoned out loud, "The demons will insert the keys into opposite slots of the altar to try and devastate Geneva's future. Perhaps you could go back to the very beginning and change the keys that they already have, so that they think they are placing them into the opposite slots, but in fact they are placing them into the correct ones."

Falcon looked at the sash that Liberty was carrying with the flowers inside.

"Perhaps this is what those Dydadem flowers are for. They do have special properties. Perhaps you are supposed to go back and use the flowers to change the keys," said Falcon

"I just have to go back far enough in time to change the keys, and go before the demons use the keys on the altar. What are we waiting for? Time is wasting!" said Liberty.

"Our time pressure is only until you jump into the river. Once you are flowing down time, there will be no rush because you will end up in a place way before this mission even begins. It's settled then. We just have to get you to that river. We'll use the river entrance at the Pinnacles of Knowledge where you were briefed, and we'll catch a light tunnel to get there," said Falcon.

"Well then, that's enough talk. Let's go!" Liberty responded.

22

ᴅᴀʀᴋɴᴇss

- mission Liberty -

Falcon and Liberty pushed hard up the mountainside to get to the nearest light tunnel.

Liberty was breathing hard and sweating by the time Falcon said, "It's just up ahead."

Suddenly band of demons descended on the two. Liberty and Falcon both drew swords.

"We don't have time for this!" said Falcon. Liberty, who was by this time angry that her mission kept being hindered, launched into full battle mode. She jumped off a rock and forcefully brought the blade of her sword down through the skull of the closest demon.

"Watch out! Crossbow!" yelled Falcon who saw that the demons were focussing most of their attention on the girl. The demon fired, but Liberty deflected the arrow with the armour plate on her forearm. Falcon flew high into the sky and came swooping down, knocking three demons to the ground at once and finishing them off with the slice of his blade.

"Can you see it?" he yelled, pointing with his sword.

Liberty looked in the direction of his sword and could faintly see the tunnel. Suddenly a flash went through it and two angels appeared with javelins in their hands. They both hurled them and pinned two demons to the ground.

"We have backup," called Falcon. "Get to the tunnel. Take the third left. Once you are in the air, take fifth right, count to three and roll out."

Liberty repeated what Falcon had said in her mind, 'Third left, fifth right, roll on three.'

"Got it!" she called.

"Watch out!" Falcon called out.

Liberty looked up and quickly dived as an arrow hit the metal plate on her thigh. It knocked the sash onto the ground and damaged her armour. "

"Are you okay?" yelled Falcon.

"Yes," she responded, as she ran over to pick up the sash with the flowers.

"Go, go, go!" said Falcon earnestly.

Liberty dashed for the tunnel. She ran past the two angels who continued to have javelins appear in their hands. As they were hurling them, the demons were slowly reducing in number. Liberty got near to the tunnel and dived in. Immediately she shot along the ground, head-first, at a blinding pace. One!

'Oh that was one.' Two whisked past. 'Focus, focus, focus.'

"Three, there it is. Turn!" she commanded herself. Liberty rolled into the tunnel on her left as it branched off. She continued to pass more branches, but waited until she felt the rise. No problem there, because suddenly she shot upwards vertically.

"One, two, three" She waited. "Four, five, turn right!" She threw herself to the right.

"Oh, two, three," and threw herself to the left and rolled completely out of the light tunnel and found herself skidding along the dark marble surface of the pinnacle.

"Yikes! Slow me down." She spread out her arms and legs and slowly came to a stop, then sat up. She turned to see Falcon sliding across the floor, but on his feet.

"What?! How do you do that?" she said twisting to look behind her, leaning on her hands, with her legs still out in front.

"Takes practice," said Falcon.

"Whatever," Liberty responded.

Falcon smiled and urged, "To the river."

The two ran over to the edge of the pinnacle.

"It is invisible from here, but this is where the river flows into the past. You will need to exit at the time the keys were formed, and use the Dydadem flowers to change the keys to look like the opposite key. Just speak to the keys in faith, while holding the flowers out, and command them to change in appearance," instructed Falcon.

"How will I know when to get out," asked Liberty.

"At the flood," Falcon responded.

"What, the actual?" said Liberty who couldn't quite believe that she would be traversing thousands of years.

"Yes, for two reasons. Firstly, many things changed during the flood. As the earth was being reformed, many altars and keys were set up for many cities. Geneva was one of those cities. The other reason is that the time river looks very similar throughout the passages of time. But at the flood, the river widens into a gulf, and this is your indicator to get out as soon as you get there."

"Got it," said Liberty.

"How will I find the keys? asked Liberty.

"I don't know," said Falcon. "All I know is they will be there, and somehow you must find them. The Holy Spirit will guide you."

Liberty stepped forward to the edge, "So I just jump off do I?" she asked.

"Yes, but you might want to take a run up," said Falcon.

"Oh! A run up? You mean I could miss the river? You do know I'm jumping off a cliff into nothingness?"

"Yes," Falcon replied. "But the river is there… pretty sure. Just try and stay afloat… and relax," he added with a smile.

"Pretty sure?"

"Positive," responded Falcon.

"Ha, just relax!" Liberty said to herself. "It's just a leap of faith."

Liberty didn't feel all that reassured, but this is what she was here for, and she felt that she did have faith for the task. She turned and walked away from the edge to give herself a runup. Then without thinking twice, she turned and sprinted towards the edge, then launched herself into the air. Liberty spread her arms in a graceful dive and suddenly entered the noisy tunnel. She could see the water rushing below her. She brought her arms together straight over her head. Breaking the surface, she plunged into the water. Submerged, she arched her back, and swam toward the surface. Her head emerged from the water and she took a breath. The water was refreshing. Liberty maneuvered her body into a feet-first position and was whisked down river.

As Liberty floated over the rapids, she fixed her eyes ahead, but with her peripheral vision, she could see the landscape that she was being carried through. Towns, and fields, and centuries of civilization. She was carried for a long time, waiting for the river to expand into the flood.

Suddenly up ahead, she saw a huge wave which was so high that she could see nothing beyond it. Liberty took a deep breath as the wave rolled over the top of her. At the same time she felt a tremendous current pull her down and shoot her forward. Liberty told herself to remain calm. She crossed her arms over her chest, and relaxed, to let the current pull her along. As she was carried, breath didn't seem to run out. It was like God was breathing into her lungs while she was underwater. Keeping her eyes open, through the clear water she could see the sky above her rushing past. Clouds whisked by at great speed.

She was quite close to the surface now, but stayed under for as long as she could hold her breath, to allow the water to take her. As she felt her lungs tightening, she pushed down with her hands to lift her body, then broke through the surface with a gasp. She breathed hard and looked around. Jungles and forests were now shooting past her.

After some time, Liberty noticed that the river was widening.

"I must be nearly here," she thought. She allowed her boots to drop down, tipping her body over from her back to her front and started swimming closer toward the riverbank. Keeping close to the edge, she noticed the bank on the other side of the river quickly receding into the distance. Liberty decided that now was the time. She swam hard for the edge, using all of her energy. Rocks were periodically scattered along the bank and Liberty grabbed hold of one of them. She used her remaining strength to hoist herself up on to it. She then stood to her feet. Liberty then jumped from rock to rock, over the remaining water, and up onto the narrow riverbank. She turned to gaze out over the waters. From the height of the riverbank, she could see the vast expanse of water in front of her. She was definitely at the place.

"This is the flood!" she thought.

The tunnel was now no longer a tunnel, but a vast canopy that disappeared in all directions, as far as the eye could see.

Liberty then turned her back on the waters, and toward the glassy wall.

'I wonder if I can just put my head through,' she thought. Liberty gave it a try. With her feet still on the bank of the time river, she stepped right up to the glassy wall and pushed her head through.

All was blackness.

'Wow,' she thought. 'I can't see a thing!'

But then, through some kind of supernatural intervention, she could suddenly see in the darkness. Even though she could see no source of light, she found that she could make out moving shapes.

It didn't seem like water, but like waves of darkness. She was standing on a shoreline, and in front of her a sea that invoked fear and chaos. She felt that if she stepped into it she would be washed away forever, tumbled about in waves that had no rhythm or sequence. The waves washed back and forth. Darkness without design, disorder without limits. As she looked, suddenly the watery darkness was drawn away from her like a tidal wave drawing in all the water to itself before making landfall. The darkness was drawn back endless miles, then it rushed at her, causing her eyes to open wide. With terrifying speed the wave surged forward, driven by an immense amount of pressure behind it. She felt that the wave would cover her and half the realm. But when it was almost upon her, it immediately halted on the shoreline, forbidden to cross over. Certainly, to step off the edge of this realm would mean being lost forever, never to come back again.

Then the voice spoke, "Step out."

23

ᎠᎪᎳᏗᏁᎥᏁᏀ

- ᎻᎥssᎥᎣᏁ ᏞᎥᏴᎬᏒᏣᎩ -

"What! No way! I'll drown," exclaimed Liberty. "I'll be submerged, wrapped in liquid darkness, unable to breathe. I'll be as a single grain of sand swept along intercontinental ocean currents, tumbled across the bed of the deepest sea, forever lost, and forever forgotten."

"You are safe with me. Come with me, I want to show you something," said the voice

"But there's nothing out there God," said Liberty, in an exasperated voice. "There is nothing but darkness and liquid void!"

"You are right. Okay, you don't have to come with me then," responded the voice in a matter-of-fact way.

"What?! No, wait!" said Liberty fearfully, who did not expect God to answer like that. She was now feeling like she was about to miss out on something amazing. This response from God was more surprising than the first command, to step out. She had expected God to keep offering until she gave in. But in fact God was allowing her to make the decision.

'It must be pretty spectacular if he is calling me out,' thought Liberty. 'But this fearful liquid mass is so vast and scary.'

"Okay God, I'm coming," she said.

"I'll enable you to walk on the waters. You won't drown," said the strong and comforting voice of God.

Liberty looked out and remembered Peter walking on the water, and so decided to completely trust the Lord. She took a big step into the liquid and was immediately drawn out the distance of a football field off-shore. It was like being caught in a strong rip that dragged her through the waves. As she stood on the waters, being drawn further and further out, waves broke over her legs and midsection. It was thicker than water, but no residue was left on her as the waves swept by. By now she was so far out that she was completely surrounded by waters endlessly in all directions. There was no sign of the shore and no point of reference. The sounds of breakers and the sloshing of waves filled her ears. The empty smell of a cold open cave swirled around her like a wind. The wind had no direction, it just was.

"What's here God?!" she called out, lifting her voice above the background roar of waves.

"Nothing yet," said God, with what sounded like a smile in his voice. It was like God was enjoying the thrill of the environment.

"Are you enjoying this?!" questioned Liberty.

"I'm enjoying seeing what is to come. Do you know where you are yet?"

"I'm at the flood," said Liberty.

"No," came the response.

'I'm not at the flood!' Liberty thought in alarm. "Then where am I?!" she yelled.

No response.

Liberty yelled again, "I'm in a place with no signpost, no landmark, no frame of reference at all, standing on some alien sea unlike anything I have ever known. So, no, I don't know where I am!"

"You have one frame of reference," said God.

"Oh yeah, what's that?" Liberty responded.

"What you have read," came the response.

"Read where?" questioned Liberty

No answer.

"Ha. I have to work it out again," said Liberty into the emptiness.

As Liberty pondered the books she read, and of course the Bible, it suddenly dawned on her.

'No! This can't be Genesis 1:1!' she thought in complete amazement.

"Have I arrived at the dawning of time?" she said in wonder.

"Hasn't started yet," said God. "I'll introduce time with the introduction of light. It's pitch black at this moment."

"You don't have to tell me that. So, how can I see?" asked Liberty.

"You are discerning all this, not using your natural eyes," God responded.

"Oh," thought Liberty. "Makes sense. So what am I here to see? Or rather, what am I here to discern?"

"You won't need to discern it, you will see it all right," came the reply. Then with a powerful, awesome voice that filled the universe, God commanded, "Let there be light!"

And there was light! A sheet of light thundered across the heavens from one end to the other. Blackness receded in all directions. The oily liquid became clear waters. The sudden brightness and clarity around her was terribly frightening because she could now see that beneath her boots was an endless expanse of water. She was standing on clear liquid with no life-vest or anything to hold on to. She had never felt so out of control, feeling that she could sink at any moment and plunge downwards to the endless watery depths.

'This is far more scary,' she thought. 'If I had a phobia of being in small places, I would totally convert to having a phobia of massive places!' Seeing the endless miles of glassy water below interrupted her breathing. She was still on her first gasp. 'Breathe, Liberty, breathe. He won't let me sink.'

Below her, the waters endlessly refracted colours and rainbows, but above her the sky was a single bright sheet, with no other detail, just flat and bright.

It took some unknown amount of time standing on the waters to allow the peace of God to fill her heart. 'If I was going to drown, it would have already happened,' she thought.

Liberty began to feel at home, but still amazed by her surroundings. She took a few steps and spun around.

Then God's thunderous voice rang out, "Let there be a vault between the waters to separate water from water."

Suddenly the waters surged upwards, totally engulfing her. She didn't know if she was falling or the waters were rising. The surge was so great that she had to close her eyes, and scrunch her face. Her arms were forced upwards and she allowed herself to become like a pin. She felt the presence of God all around her, so there was no need to fear. The breath of God filled her lungs, allowing her to relax into the experience. The upsurge of water continued and Liberty knew that God was giving her supernatural breath to enable her to remain submerged for as long as it took for this next transformation to take place. Miles and miles of water and bubbles gushed around her.

Suddenly she was washed into mid-air. Liberty opened her eyes. Looking up, she saw a swirling canopy of blue, and felt the rain falling onto her face. She then looked below and saw the watery sea far below, but she didn't fall. Liberty was suspended in mid-air, in the midst of a heavy downpour, raining all around her. It felt warm, it felt like an atmosphere.

She just hung for an unknown period of time. As the rain eased she heard the words, "Let the water under the sky be gathered to one place, and let dry ground appear."

Then there was great movement in the waters. Dark patches from the deeps got larger and larger. Suddenly in an explosion of waters, the land erupted from the depths. Bare rock rose to form landmasses. Far below her everything had movement, and there were enormous bursts of water. The scale of the transformations made her feel as small as a single drop in the ocean. Again she left to observe in wonder for an unknown period of time.

Then God said, "Let the land produce vegetation: seed-bearing plants and trees on the land that bear fruit with seed in it, according to their various kinds."

Then, an amazing movement of growth on the land sprung up. Grasses, flowers, plants and trees covered the land until all was various shades of green with pops of colour gracing the countryside.

It was amazing to see the creative landscape taking shape below her. Suddenly God's voice boomed out, "Let there be lights in the vault of the sky to separate the day from the night, and let them serve as signs to mark sacred times, and days and years, and let them be lights in the vault of the sky to give light on the earth."

Stars were scattered over the skies, and then the sun was made, and also the moon. As Liberty watched, the earth beneath her began to spin. The entire world was shown to her as she circumnavigated the globe. One thing she noticed as she was gliding past the continents, was bright shining points on the surface. The globe then slowed its spin and came to rest with her directly above what would be Switzerland. She noticed a shining point directly below her as she was lowered to the surface. Liberty landed in a clearing with long grass. All around was vegetation and plants, but yet no animals.

"Are these what you are after?" said God.

In front of here were two bright shining keys suspended in mid-air spinning around each other.

"Are these the keys to Geneva?" she asked, still looking at them.

"Yes," came the response.

Liberty looked around, but could not see the form of God.

"Can I take these?" she said.

"No," said God. "But I have brought you here for a reason, because you have brought something with you."

"I have?" Liberty responded.

"Take the flowers from within your sash and hold them out towards the keys," God instructed.

Liberty reached into her sash and found that only two flowers remained.

'Two flowers, and two keys,' she thought. 'Meant to be.'

Liberty held up the flowers and they were lifted from her hand.

They floated away and were caught up in the midst of the spinning of the keys. The bright keys started to drip liquid light. As the droplets fell toward the ground below, they had sudden changes of direction. Before hitting the ground, they shot sideways and down, as if hitting a surface. The droplets traced out the edges of an object beneath the keys.

"Oh, it's the altar," said Liberty. As the liquid light continued to fall, the edges of the altar became clear. The altar itself remained invisible, but as the droplets raced along the edges, the shape of it became distinguishable, including the slots on the top that the two keys belonged to.

Then in the midst of the golden rain, the flowers descend to rest on the top of the altar. As they touched the surface the two slots spun around each other to swap places. Once the transition was complete, and the framework had been set, the droplets fell thicker and faster and started to fill the body of the altar. It was shaped like a steep pyramid, cut off at the top to form a flat surface with the slots at each end. At the base of the altar, three steps extended out on each side to touch the ground.

Then as the droplets eased off, and the trails of gold fell to the ground, what remained was a magnificent stone structure. It was beautifully crafted and already looked ancient, even though it had just been created. This was an altar that was fit to have a city built around it.

The keys then continued to spin above the altar as they had before.

"Wow!" exclaimed Liberty. "What an amazing thing to witness the creation of the altar of Geneva."

"You have done well. Now you will be sent back, to be with your friends again," said God.

Liberty blurted out, "But I want to stay. I want to see more…"

It was too late, all around her became blurry, out of focus. Liberty felt dizzy. The earth was leaving her, or she was leaving the earth. At least she was leaving that time. All faded out to nothing and all around was empty. Then there was a rush, but unlike before. Liberty was being guided through the river in the palm of God's hand. She was gliding faster than the current, like a ship with a sail, carried by God himself. Then she was lifted and fuzzy shapes appeared around her. A landscape, a place began to form around her, and she found herself on the shore of the lake.

24

ᴅᴇᴘᴛʜꜱ

- ᴍɪꜱꜱɪᴏɴ ɢɪʀʟꜱ -

Samantha, Layla, and Trinity felt bungyed into existence like an elastic rope had pulled them out of freefall and onto the ground.

"Wow, that was crazy!" said Trinity, taking a moment feel normal again. Then she said, "Glad we didn't go splat… which means the fun has only just begun!"

"Yes, I am glad we survived that in one piece," responded Layla, checking to make sure that the other two hadn't suffered any ill effects after the fall.

"What a beautiful place," said Samantha.

The girls found themselves amongst trees, on top of a hill with long grass sprouting in clumps between the rocks. Bird songs could be heard from the tops of trees, along with the buzzing of insects around them. The forest felt alive. They spread out to explore their surroundings.

"Up here," called Trinity. The other two joined her as she pointed.

Between the trees they could see the lake a long way off, glistening in the sun. "That's where we're headed," she said.

"Nice," responded Layla. "Hey Sam, you're looking good in your kit."

The three checked out their armour and weapons.

Layla drew a bow, aiming at a tree in the distance and released, directly hitting the centre of the trunk.

"Nice shot!" said Trinity. "Is that the one you were aiming for?" she asked smiling.

"Oh shut up!" responded Layla with a smile. "If I'd been aiming at a different tree, I would have hit a different tree."

"Ouch," said Trinity. "Demons watch out!"

The three turned toward the lake and skipped down the hill, and into the forest.

They picked their way through the forest, between the trees as shafts of light broke through the leafy canopy above.

"Quick, hide," said Layla suddenly in a hushed tone. The three split and found cover. Layla and Samantha crouched next to each other, while Trinity crouched next to a tree on the other side of the path.

"What is it?" whispered Samantha.

"I felt a breeze. A presence," said Layla.

Just then, behind them was a snapping of twigs. Layla looked up to see a creature striding toward them in full armour, with a sword in each hand. It was a huge warrior. Unsure if it had seen them, Layla looked over at Trinity and started to motion with her hands. Trinity got the message, 'I'll create a distraction, and you attack.'

Unsure if the message got through, but with no time to make sure,

Layla stood battle-ready, revealing her position. The creature turned its head and stopped in its tracks to examine the trespasser. Layla backed away, drawing its attention from where Trinity was hiding.

Layla drew an arrow and shot at the creature. Trinity quickly sprung up from her position behind the monster, and unsheathed her sword. She stepped up onto a rock, then jumped, gripping her sword with both hands she plunged it into its back. Trinity remained holding the sword while being flung around, as the creature tried to reach behind. It then looked for a tree to back into to crush Trinity. Layla strung another arrow, and released a silver-tipped arrow which hit the creature and sunk deep into the its body. Trinity let go of her sword and dropped to the ground, before being smashed into a tree trunk. Samantha rushed forward to launch another assault, and plunged her sword into the creature's torso. The beast hit the tree behind, and ricocheted off, dropping to its knees. It fell flat on its face, and flaked apart into ash as it hit the ground. Then, as if the dark realms were drawing it home, the ash was gathered up in a wind and taken away.

The girls who were panting and staring at each other with wide eyes, suddenly broke into laughter, relieved that the situation had ended as it did.

"You are lethal," Layla said to Trinity.

"We smoked it together," Trinity said with a wink, picking up her sword from the ground. Fortunately the demon blood had also flaked away, leaving her sword still clean and shining.

"There are probably more," said Layla. "We need to be careful."

They continued to cautiously make their way through the forest, then noticed more movement up ahead. Again they crouched down, then listened hard.

"Sounds like a lot of them up ahead," said Trinity. "We need a better look."

The three crept closer until they could see a line of warriors, much like the one they had just killed. The line stretched out before them as far as they could see. There was also a faint purple glow which pulsed between them creating a wall or barricade of some sort.

"They're blocking the path to the lake," said Samantha. "Perhaps they know we are coming."

The girls retreated to a safe distance to consider their options.

"Over here," called Trinity, motioning with her hand. The other two followed. Trinity walked toward the mouth of a cave.

"Let's hide out here until we figure out what to do," Layla suggested.

They cautiously looked in. The end of the cave was shrouded in darkness, but it felt safe enough at the entrance.

"What do you think?" asked Layla. "Do we fight our way through from here, or continue along the forest until we find a gap in the ranks?"

There was a long pondering silence.

"Well we can't just look at each other and do nothing. I'm going to check out the back of this cave and see how far it goes," said Trinity.

"Just be careful," replied Layla.

Trinity started to walk toward the back of the cave, staying alert to the slightest sound. She drew her sword just in case. As the light dimmed she felt a soft breeze against her skin. As she walked deeper, the armour on her forearm started to glow, responding to the lack of light. The deeper she got the brighter her armour glowed.

'Amazing!" she thought. "What clever armour."

Trinity glanced back. The bright entrance was further away than she had expected. She could see the silhouette of Layla and Samantha talking with each other. Trinity felt that she had gone far enough without them, so she turned back to get her friends.

Meanwhile the other two were talking at the entrance. Then looking up and pointing toward the top of the mouth of the cave. Layla said, "It looks like carving up on the top."

"Too much grass and moss to see what it is, but it looks like words to me. Let's go up and see if we can clear it," said Samantha.

The two scrambled up the side of the cave and started pulling off moss and dirt and grass, allowing it to drop to the ground below. They worked hard uncovering the inscription. As Trinity worked down the right hand side, she exclaimed, "Oh it's a Bible verse. This is the reference, Job 28:10-11."

Once it was clear enough to read they got down and were joined by Trinity who had emerged from her exploration. The inscription was mostly clear and so Samantha read it out. "They tunnel through the rock; their eyes see all its treasures. They search the sources of the rivers and bring hidden things to light. Job 28:10-11"

"It's like an invitation," said Layla. "What did you find in there?" she asked, turning to Trinity.

"It just kept going. There was also a gentle breeze, indicating that there's another opening to the surface somewhere in the cave system, giving it a transient atmosphere. And the really cool thing is that my armour glowed the deeper I got, so that I could see."

"I think that's our path," said Trinity. "The verse talks about 'the sources of the rivers' which are either springs or lakes. I think that this will take us behind the enemy lines toward the lake. You guys up for it?"

"I'm willing to be led by a verse from the Bible," said Samantha smiling. "Let's do it."

The three once again turned toward the darkness of the cave. Layla held out her hands to the others to take hold of. She squeezed their hands and prayed, "Lord, lead us." They then dropped their grasp and ventured forth.

As the light around them grew dimmer, their armour started to glow. With the three of them together there was enough of a glow to light their way. The cave continued on and on. Trinity led the way, cautiously placing her steps. As the cave was narrowing, Trinity said, "Looks like we've got a bit of climbing to do."

She stepped up onto a rock and squeezed her body through the narrow gap. "A bit tight," she said.

Layla was feeling a little claustrophobic, thinking, 'Here we are, squeezing through dark narrow gaps under tonnes of earth and rock. Our bare hands assaulting the flinty rock, trespassing through deep pathways, uncovering secret passages. God, keep us safe.'

Just up ahead Trinity dropped down and Layla heard a splash. "Are you alright?" she called.

"Yes, fine," came the echoey response. "We've got some water here."

The three got through the tight section and found themselves in ankle deep water. As they continued deeper into the cave system, the water got deeper and deeper. Eventually the cold water got to waist height.

"We could always turn back," suggested Samantha.

"We could," Trinity responded. "But to what? We've got nowhere else to go. I think we need to keep pushing ahead until we can go no further.

"That may not be too far away," said Layla. "Looks like the cave ends just up ahead."

The three got to where the cave finished, now standing in water just above their waist.

"Can't be the end," said Trinity. "There must be another way. It can't just finish."

"The water must come from somewhere," said Samantha. "The cave probably continues, but submerged."

"I'm going to check it out," said Trinity.

"You can't be serious!" responded Layla. 'You mean under the water?"

"Wish me luck," she responded, and with that took a deep breath and plunged beneath the water. From above Samantha and Layla could track her watery glow. Then it disappeared.

25

ĐIAMONĐS

- MISSION GIRLS -

Moments later Trinity appeared again gasping for breath.

"You girl, are hard core!" exclaimed Layla.

"Ha, I thought I had better go before I over-thought it," Trinity puffed, running her hands over her face and hair to wipe off the water. "Anyway my hand broke the surface on the other side. I didn't go all the way, but wanted to come back and take a deeper breath. It's not far, but I think we can continue on the other side. I'm going again."

With that she disappeared and did not re-emerge.

After half a minute came a muffled call, "Hey, can you hear me?"

"Yes, we can," Samantha shouted back.

"It opens up over here. It's massive!" said Trinity.

"We're coming," shouted Layla.

"We can do this," Samantha said to Layla holding her hand.

"Yes, we can," Layla responded. "You go first. I'll come after."

Samantha took a deep breath and dropped down beneath the

surface. She pushed forward and her glow disappeared.

After a short time, Layla shouted, "Did you make it?" She listened hard.

"Yes," came the response. "It's not far."

Layla composed herself, took a breath, then plunged beneath the cold water. Immediately water poured in through her armour, drenching her completely. She pushed forward with her eyes open and arms outstretched. She could see the glow of the other two above her on the other side. Layla swam hard, and reached for the surface. She erupted from the water with a gasp.

"Good on you!" applauded Trinity. The three hugged as Layla was catching her breath.

"Let's push on," suggested Samantha. "We don't want our core to get cold."

The three waded through the water, disturbing the hidden passages of deep darkness; beneath the roots of mountains, getting further and further away from above-surface dwellings.

"I'm glad there are no other signs of life here like spiders," said Layla, from the back as they continued.

"Or demons," added Samantha.

Then Trinity said from the front, "Can you guys feel the change in atmosphere? It's like the air is feeling thicker."

"I think it's a sound," said Samantha. "Like a gentle hum."

"Yes, you're right," said Layla, "and it's getting louder."

"Another tight squeeze here," Trinity said, pushing her body through the gap. Then adding, "Wow!"

"What?!" asked Samantha.

The three emerged into a cavern which sparkled in the glow of their armour.

"Diamonds!" whispered Samantha in awe. "This place is full of them. This is where the hum is coming from. It's like the diamonds are singing."

The three slowly stepped out into the cavern and spread out, looking all around in amazement at the beauty of the diamond garden. The sound of crunching diamonds under their feet made them feel like trespassers, disturbing the equilibrium. As they got into the middle of the cavern. Trinity said, "I feel a definite breeze coming from my right. It could be our way out." She turned to walk in the direction of the breeze, still admiring the display of the twinkling lights of the underground night sky. A lost sister to the stars above, having been transformed by the fires below.

As Trinity was about to lead them out of the cavern and venture into the next tunnel, she said, "I was thinking about the inscription on the mouth of the cave, '…their eyes see all its treasures… and bring hidden things to light.' Do you think we should pocket some diamonds, and take them with us to the surface, 'bringing hidden things to light'?"

"I guess we could," responded Samantha. "Surely we are here for a reason. I would hate to take what we shouldn't take, but there are some loose ones here on the ground." Samantha reached down and selected a couple of diamonds of various sizes to take with her.

Trinity saw one she liked, and she reached down, but it wouldn't come away easily. She gave it a tug and it came free in her hand. Then suddenly there was the sound of a crack. As they looked around, multiple fracture lines appeared in the walls of the cavern and diamonds started breaking away and showering down upon them.

"Quick, run!" shouted Layla as diamonds pinged off their armour.

"Watch out!" yelled Samantha, grabbing hold of Layla and pulling her out of the way of a chunk of deadly glistening rock smashing down onto the ground in front of her.

Samantha and Layla both dropped the diamonds from their hands in their efforts to dodge the deadly falling shards.

As Trinity rushed ahead toward their exit, a piece of wall broke off, blocking their way.

"Quick, look for another way," Trinity shouted.

"Yes, over here," responded Samantha. "I think I see another way out!"

The three girls rushed through the deadly glassy rain, amidst the sound of deafening cracks.

"In here, quick," called Samantha, helping the other two into the tunnel. Within the relative safety of a tunnel of bare rock, they turned to see the cavern imploding in on itself, shaking the ground where they were standing.

"Let's keep going, and get a safe distance away," urged Layla. The girls hurried through the tunnel to a place where they felt safe to rest.

After some heavy breathing Samantha said, "I dropped the diamonds I had."

"Yeah, me too," said Layla.

"I got one," said Trinity, who then burst out laughing from relief. "I'm just glad we are not dead, and that at least we have one diamond to show for our adventures."

"Such a shame to have all that beauty destroyed," said Samantha, making a sad face.

"I know," Layla responded. "Hope it doesn't turn out to be a big mistake."

"You know," said Trinity, "perhaps the tunnel we were going to take was going to be the mistake, and the collapse directed us to this one instead. I'd like to think that God has his eye on us. What's done is done. Let's just keep in faith for what lies ahead."

"Too true," responded Layla. "We had better keep going."

The cave system continued for a long way. The explorers slowly trekked through the recesses of the depths, illuminating ancient darkness. Every so often they would sit to take a break and then continue through the uncharted cavities of the earth.

"I think we are getting close," Trinity finally said. "We are climbing upwards and the air smells fresher."

The cave widened and the three emerged into a moonlit forest. The air was still warm from the heat of the day, and all was quiet and still.

"Let's find a place to sleep tonight. Just inside the cave here is probably good."

The girls were tired and quickly drifted off to sleep.

26

CRYSTAL CITY
- MISSION GIRLS -

Layla lay asleep, dreaming…

She walked through the smouldering ruins. Ash hung in the air and a soft blanket of grey covered the snowy ground. Pillars of smoke towered above her while flames lit up the mountains in the distance. Suddenly another bright trail of smoke fell from the sky, hurtling toward the earth. It shot through the sky high above her, then the dull thud of it landing in the distance caused the ground to tremble. The clouds above her were illuminated with pockets of light, and fiery stars burst through the cloud-cover. Scriptures came to mind, 'His tail swept down a third of the stars of heaven and cast them to the earth.' Smoke filled the air around her and she sneezed.

"What? Smoke?" she said groggily. waking up. She lifted herself onto her elbow.

"Good morning," said a familiar male voice.

"What the…?!"

"Making you some breakfast."

Layla sat up fully, rubbed her face and said, "Trillion, how did you get here? And how long have you been here?"

"You hungry or not?" asked Trillion.

"You just decide to turn up and make breakfast?!" exclaimed Layla.

"You'll need it for the next part of your journey," responded Trillion.

Layla groaned and said to herself out load, "I've just woken up from a crazy dream. Now an angel is making me breakfast!"

She sat for a few moments longer, then rose from where she had been lying and stood to her feet. The others began to stir as well.

"What's happening Layla?" asked Samantha in a semi-sleep, semi-awake state.

"Well, we have an angel over here cooking over an open fire, asking if we want breakfast," responded Layla.

"Just say 'yes' for me," said Samantha, still lying on her back with her eyes closed.

Layla, then turned back to Trillion and said, "It's good to see you anyway. Did you know we have already killed a massive warrior demon, tunnelled through the heart of the earth, and narrowly avoided being crushed and buried never to be seen again?"

"Really?! I didn't know that," responded Trillion, with a look of concern.

"Oh, it's fine," said Layla rolling her eyes. "Anyway, why didn't we get any angel help? And why couldn't we have been dropped here, instead of way back beyond where all the demons had created the roadblock?"

"Exactly!" said Trillion. "That isn't just a single roadblock, it's a perimeter. The enemy is being very cautious and has set up a massive perimeter around Crystal City. Any disturbance within the perimeter would be detected. A disturbance such as dropping three humans into the realm. They don't want humans trying to restore the throne."

"Makes sense," said Layla. Samantha and Trinity were now also listening in to the conversation.

"That's why you needed to walk in. To be honest, I didn't know how you would get through, but I did know that the Holy Spirit would guide you," Trillion said.

"Well, we got through using the cave system and came out here," said Samantha.

"I didn't know there was a cave system," came the sound of another familiar voice.

"Seraph... and Shar!" exclaimed Samantha, as the both of them appeared from the forest walking towards the group.

"We've just come from assignment, but are here to help you now," said Shar. "Why don't you three have breakfast, then we can get ready to go to the lake."

***

As the girls were eating, Trinity said to Shar, "Seeing as we are here, having breakfast, why don't you tell me about some of your adventures."

"Adventures?" exclaimed Shar. "I don't know if you'd call them adventures, we have missions and assignments."

"Do you get any down-time? You know, just to relax. Or is it always serious for you guys?" asked Samantha.

Shar looked across at Trillion and Seraph with a smile, and said "Hey, Samantha wants to know if it's always serious, or if we have fun too!"

Seraph nudged Shar, "Tell them what you did with that rock when things were being set up."

"Oh, don't bring that up again," responded Shar. "They don't want to know about that."

"Yes we do!" said Trinity. "Tell us."

"Hmmm," said Shar. "I don't know if I should tell you, but I guess there's no harm in it. There are many things that humans are best not to know about, but this one is probably safe enough."

Shar paused, as if checking in with God, then continued, "It was back when things were being birthed. We were involved in setting up the solar system and the Milky Way galaxy, and all of that. I was working on some stars in a nearby part of the galaxy and picked up a piece of space rock. I then decided, on a whim, to fling it towards the sun," he said, with a somewhat sheepish expression.

"And," encouraged Trinity.

"I wasn't supposed to interfere with earth's solar system, but I just kind of did it anyway. I'm a good aim and of course wasn't trying to hit the sun or the earth. So, now it happens to be caught in an orbit and it flies past the earth every 75 years," he said.

"What?!" exclaimed Trinity. "You are not literally talking about Halley's Comet! You set up Halley's Comet?"

Shar didn't respond.

"And you didn't ask permission?" asked Trinity again in disbelief.

"No, but when God saw what I had done, he quite liked it and commended me for the idea," Shar quickly added.

Trinity burst out laughing. "Halley's Comet was just a joke. Ha-ha, what an awesome story. Don't tell me that the other planets in our solar system were just created on a whim too."

"Oh, no. Very intentional, all the planets… except Uranus," said Shar.

"No, you can't be serious!" said Trinity, who was having the time of her life, hearing stories of angels fooling around and making their own mark on creation.

"God did put the planet itself there, but the ring got added after," said Shar.

"How?!" Trinity burst out, totally engrossed in the back story of the solar system. Layla and Samantha were also leaning in on the conversation with big smiles on their faces.

"We were holding a celebration in heaven, and one of the angels, Thunderclap, thought it would be a great idea to give Uranus a vertical stripe and present it to God like a gift-wrapped planet. God thought it was very creative. But he ended up scrubbing the coloured stripe off the surface giving it an orbital ring instead. He kept it vertical as a reminder."

By this stage Trinity was lying on her back laughing out loud, looking up at the blue cloudless sky.

"There's always a chance to rest and have fun, even in the middle of a serious mission," said Seraph.

"You guys are awesome," Samantha replied.

***

After an extremely good breakfast the girls rose, excited for the next part of their adventure.

"Ready?" asked Trillion who was shovelling earth over the fire to put it out.

"Ready!" responded Layla.

The six ventured into the forest again towards the lake which was still some distance away.

After an hour or so of walking, they emerged at the edge of the waters.

What was a plain wide open expanse across the surface of the lake to a natural observer, was anything but plain in the spirit realm. Before them was a spectacular glass city that shone brightly in the sunlight, and reflected the clouds above. Beautifully formed towers rose up out of the water, each different from the other, but all cohesive in design, perfectly integrated with each other.

High above the waters, parts of the city were built on floating islands that hung in the air. Interconnecting walkways linked towers and elegant crystal structures. The vast spire-sprinkled skyline looked well established as if it had stood for centuries, but the clean lines and delicate architecture gave it the qualities of a new-build, as if it had been completed just yesterday.

A glassy causeway extended across the lake, from the shore into the main entrance of the city. There was much activity. Angels and demons were walking back and forth along the causeway. Groups were also walking along the many levels of skyways across Crystal City.

They could also see that there was just as much activity under the water as there was above it. The city extended beneath the surface of the lake with clear tubes serving as transport passages. connecting underwater structures.

"Isn't it amazing?!" exclaimed Samantha.

"It a sky city and an underwater city at the same time," said Layla.

"And the throne is in the midst of all that somewhere," said Trinity.

"So what do we do? Where's the throne?" asked Layla

"The throne has been damaged," Trillion responded. "The demons have broken pieces off it. You need to collect the pieces and bring them together.

"The throne itself is in the main courtyard in the middle of the city. The enemy tried to destroy the throne, but they could not. So they dismantled it instead, breaking parts of it off. There are three of you, and there are three parts of the throne that need to be recovered and fitted back into place.

"One part lies beneath the waters. The enemy has discarded it at the bottom of the lake, thinking that no one would find it there. But one of our lookouts saw the piece being dropped. Samantha, you will search for that piece.

"Layla, you will retrieve the second part which is in one of the spires of the citadel. One of the high ranking demons decided to keep that part for itself amongst its collection of other relics.

"Trinity, you will need to search amongst the dungeons for the final piece. We are not exactly sure where that piece is, but we do know that it is somewhere within Crystal City on one of the lower levels. The dungeons are the best place to start."

Seraph handed to each a medallion which could be strapped to their wrist.

"These medallions are made of throne material," said Seraph. "When they are in close proximity to the other parts of the throne, they will glow, so you will know that you are near. When you have the pieces, get to the throne as quickly as you can."

Layla looked at her warrior friends, confident in their ability to complete their tasks.

'We got this,' she thought.

27

SUBMERGED

- mission samantha -

"**W**hen do we start?" asked Samantha.

"We will get you on your way now," Trillion replied. "You'll need this," he said, as he handed her a slim helmet. Then added, "And we will get you into a suit."

"No tanks?" asked Samantha.

"No. The helmet converts water into oxygen. The filters last only a few hours, but it should be enough time for you to locate the piece of the throne. Once you have it, a light tunnel will take you into the royal courtyard."

"Are you also getting a suit?" Samantha asked Seraph.

"No I can't come with you," Seraph responded. "I will need to help Trillion and Layla."

"Oh, I'm going alone, am I?" asked Samantha nervously. "You'd better give me good instructions."

Trillion and Seraph spent some time talking with Samantha,

getting her into the suit, and briefing her on the best route to take to the middle of the lake.

Trillion concluded by saying, "There is no reason for demons to be down there in the lake. They don't like getting wet, so you shouldn't have direct opposition. You'll have the element of surprise because they won't be expecting a human to be diving for the piece of the throne. But, be careful of being spotted from within the submerged city. They can see out into the lake, and will dispatch patrols if they have to."

Samantha walked towards the edge of the lake. As she got to the water's edge, she stopped for a moment and gazed out across the surface, admiring the busy city. She then continued to walk into the water.

It felt a little cold at first. 'I'll get used to it,' she thought.

As she got to waist-deep she turned and waved to her friends, then dived under and disappeared from view.

Samantha could see quite clearly through her visor and could hear her own breathing as she settled into a stroke rhythm. As she swam forward, following the lay of the lakebed, she could see the glow in the distance from the underwater buildings and tunnels.

As she got closer, she could see that it was just as busy under the surface as it was above. She saw mostly demons walking through the tunnels, fulfilling various duties within the rooms of Crystal City. A few angels could be seen from time to time.

She swam down towards a glassy structure and sidled up to a tubular passageway. The tunnels were mostly transparent, apart from the walkways within the tunnels. The walkways looked to be made of solid steel.

'If I swim right up close, under the steel walkways, I should be able to go unnoticed,' she thought.

Samantha pushed herself down and squeezed into the gap between the silt of the lakebed below, and the tubular passageway above. She followed the line of the tunnel, sloping ever deeper toward the middle of the lake. The tunnel above gently pressed against her back, as she let it slide along the full length of her body. Bubbles from the breathing vents in her helmet escaped from under the tunnel and rose through the water.

She neared the end of the tunnel which connected to the room in front of her. Samantha waited for an appropriate moment to dart under the room to the safety of the next tunnel on the far side. Demons were walking back and forth and she would surely be seen if she got her timing wrong. Waiting for a couple of minutes, she found her moment when the room was empty. She pushed off and swam as fast as she could to get to her next place of concealment. Samantha reached out for the tunnel ahead, and pulled herself under it. She looked back to see if she had been spotted. Just then, two demons walked into the building, but didn't even look up as they were discussing some matter between them.

Samantha continued this same strategy again and again, navigating her way ever deeper, toward the middle of the lake. Sometimes she would wait for many minutes looking for her opportunity to make the next exposed crossing.

As she swam along the underside of yet another tunnel, she had a sudden realisation, 'I must be very deep by now!' Becoming a little too aware of the vast body of water above her, compared to the small pocket of air within her helmet keeping her alive, she became briefly claustrophobic and had a mild panic attack. Urgently she spoke to herself, 'It's okay Samantha. You are just fine. This is just a part of the mission. It's going to be alright. Just swim!'

She forced herself to remain calm and allowed her mind to become at peace with her surroundings again. She looked ahead at her hands as they flowed through the darkening waters. Her hands reached out in front, made smooth arcing motions, then disappeared from slight in a repetitive cycle. The deep water was getting more hazy, and the soft glow of the city illuminated particles of silt, sand and vegetation hanging in the water. Her motions stirred the bits and pieces floating around her.

'It's like a liquid galaxy down here,' she said to herself. 'Swimming through thousands of tiny stars that would otherwise be undisturbed.' As the dust glided past her visor, Samantha felt very alone in the watery expanse.

'I'm so deep now, there's no going back even if I wanted to. I can't even remember the path I took to get here,' she thought.

Up ahead the tunnel connected to a large circular room. On the opposite side was the next tunnel that she needed to get to. This room was more populated than the others, but had a solid floor. The solid floor would conceal her, providing her bubbles didn't draw attention as they escaped up the sides of the room. The room looked like an observation area, so she decided that she would hold her breath as long as she could while swimming under it. The room was so large that she would have to take at least a few breaths.

She got to the edge of the room, took a deep breath, then launched out under the circular structure. She made wide strokes, covering the maximum distance with the least effort, so as to hold her breath for the longest amount of time.

Samantha took a breath, then another. By the time she had cleared the room, she had taken five or six breaths. Unaware whether or not her bubbles had been noticed, she had to push on. She continued to track underneath this long underpass for a long time.

Eventually Samantha came to a place where to her right, there was a chasm that broke away from the underwater city. Trillion had briefed her on this point. That chasm marked her path. As she neared her branching off point, she swum up to look around to see if there were any observers. All seemed clear, so she pushed off in the direction of the chasm.

Up until now, she had adequate light from the glow of Crystal City, but the chasm was dark. She swam down into the darkened depths. Samantha raised her hand and touched the side of her helmet. Two lights flicked on from her helmet to illuminate the underwater landscape.

Sediment stirred as she glided over the rocks and underwater plants, swaying gently in the current. She continued her descent towards the middle of the lake, pushing her way through the plants. Samantha suddenly froze as she saw a giant shadow, bulging in the waters in front of her. Immediately she switched off her lights and waited. All around was dark.

After about a minute, which felt like an hour, she reached for the lights again, but hesitated as she felt a voice in her spirit say, 'Wait.'

Samantha continued to wait. 'My oxygen is getting lower,' she thought.

Then another thought came to mind, 'Waiting is good for the soul.'

'What?' she responded to herself, that thought didn't come from me. Then, aware that she was talking to the Holy Spirit, she allowed the conversation to play out as she hugged the lakebed.

'Patiently waiting builds strength.'

'I don't want to wait down here,' she responded. 'How long do I have to wait?'

A verse came to mind, 'You too, be patient and stand firm, because the Lord's coming is near.'

'Oh, come on! That was written over a thousand years ago. And you're not coming back any time soon, at least, not while I'm on mission… in the past!' Samantha thought.

'I promise things ahead of time, giving you the soul-building opportunity to wait.'

Samantha's thoughts now turned to consider the craziness of the situation. 'I am underwater, at the bottom of Lake Geneva, on a quest to save this city. I'm also hiding from whatever giant creature is out there, the Holy Spirit takes the opportunity to give me some life lessons! It's like God is so big, he can put the mission on hold for a bit and sit me down in this underwater classroom and have a conversation, like it's just a normal thing to do.'

Samantha smiled to herself, took a deep breath of oxygen, and closed her eyes, which didn't make a difference because she couldn't see anything anyway. She stilled herself waited. As she did, she became more aware of her body, her fingers, arms, legs, toes, and became more aware of her watery weightless surroundings.

'This is a mental break from the pressure of the mission,' she thought. 'My body is weightless, and God wants my mind to be weightless as well. Even in the most intense times of life, there is an opportunity to rest in the Lord.'

In this moment, in the middle of an epic adventure to save a city, her mind drifted back to the surface, to her home, her family, her friends. She thought of her friend Chelsea who was going through a hard time with her family because her parents had split up. Samantha prayed, 'Lord, give Chelsea peace. Help her to find you. Give her an assurance that you will never leave her.' As she prayed she felt a puff of energy released from around her, and knew that her prayer had made a difference for her friend.

'I would never have thought to pray for Chelsea in the midst of a history-altering mission. You Lord are much bigger than all of this,' she thought.

'You're clear,' came the response.

'What? Clear for what?' asked Samantha, who was now feeling quite calm.

'Clear to swim. The path is clear now.'

'Oh. Right. I'll swim then,' Samantha responded.

She flicked her lights on and pushed forward again. Ahead of her, the chasm opened out into a hazy underwater lagoon. Bits and pieces of wooden and metal objects lay scattered across the surface. A cloth sack, books, discarded weapons, an upside down table, some broken chairs…

'A dumping-ground,' she thought.

Just then she noticed the medallion on her wrist start to glow.

'Excellent! I must be close,' she thought, as she swam into the open expanse, looking out for anything that looked throne-like.

Suddenly Samantha was hit hard on the back of her helmet and pushed downwards. She kicked her legs, but her boots hit the object.

Unable to swim, she sunk quickly toward the lakebed under the weight of the object.

Samantha was caught totally off-guard. One moment it was absolutely peaceful, and the next she was fighting to free herself from being crushed. She hit the pile of debris hard, and was pinned down. Samantha pushed with her hands, trying to lift the object on her back. It moved a little, but not enough to free her. She waited, gathering her strength, then she tried again, pushing as hard as she could, but was unable to dislodge her body.

'I'm trapped,' she thought, 'at the bottom of a lake with limited oxygen!'

Unable to move she started to feel helpless and desperate.

'Samantha, you are going to die down here,' came the unwelcome thought. 'You are unworthy to complete your quest.'

'Unworthy?' her mind responded. 'Am I unworthy?'

Her mind started to darken as she listened to the uninvited thoughts.

Suddenly there was movement beneath her, and the ground gave way.

"Help!" she cried, releasing a burst of bubbles. Then she fell through the lakebed, and into darkness.

The weight had lifted from off her, and now she felt no weight at all, falling through an under-realm. Then her boots touched the surface. It was solid, but not hard. It felt a little squidgy like standing on a mossy surface.

"Where am I?"

"You are in your own depression," came the shadowy whisper.

28

CASTLE

- mission samantha -

As Samantha's eyes grew more accustomed to her dim surroundings, she found herself amongst old ruins, with vegetation growing all over the stonework. The only light emanated from glowing clusters of tiny flowers scattered amongst the ancient structures. Samantha went over to look at a cluster, growing out of the dark brick work. 'What exquisite design,' she thought, admiring the blossoms.

Either side of her towered high stone walls with tree roots and vines overhanging the tops. As she walked along the pathway looking for a way out, she found an opening in one of the walls to her left and walked through it, but came to another pathway with another high wall on the other side. This time she started running, getting more desperate for a way out. She turned this way and that as she came to openings and archways, but still there were walls upon walls. The glowing clusters were quite distant from each other, some high and some low, but none indicated a way out.

Feeling helpless, Samantha stopped running and slumped down with her back to the wall and put her head in her hands.

"I want to get out," Samantha said anxiously.

"Oh no, you can't do that. You've entered the dark lands. You can't get out of here," said a voice.

"Perhaps I can't," said Samantha.

"Yes, you must stay. Stay in your depression. Stay in this place, because nobody cares about you, nobody even knows you are here," said the gloomy voice.

"That's probably true," said Samantha in response.

"Remember when you were at school, and those kids called you those names? That's who you are. You're useless."

"Yes, they were right. All those words. I am useless…" responded Samantha.

Then she paused.

"But hold on… they were just kids. They haven't seen the rest of my life. I've done some good things. At least I know that you love me Jesus," Samantha said, trying to turn her thoughts toward Jesus.

"Oh no, forget all of that. You are just as useless now as what you ever were. You aren't loved because you aren't lovable," said the voice with a nasty tone.

As the darkness was bearing down on her, she had a thought, 'But God, you made me, and weren't you there with me the whole time?'

"That's right," came another voice, a comforting strong voice. "I was there. I saw what they said, but you are not those things. You are who I say you are."

"No!" shouted the shadows. "He wasn't there. You were alone."

"I would never leave you," said the strong voice. "I was there then, and I am with you now."

Then from the depths of her soul, Samantha called out, "What do you say about me Jesus?"

That question was all that was needed for healing words from Jesus to flow:

You are captivating, unique, exclusive, rare, uncommon, stunning.

Within your eyes there is life and light and the evidence of God.

Your eyes radiate trails of glory, from the centre to the edges.

Like an expanding array of colour, dazzling threads, blazing outwards.

They are windows to your soul.

They unlock, they discern and they confound this world, revealing another realm.

There is a new world, a fresh universe.

Spiritual and eternal life are opened up.

The centre draws you deep, carries you away.

Eternity is deep and far away, but the pathway for you is uncovered.

Glimpses of light, purpose and life are seen within.

The centre uncovers your thoughts, exposes his image.

Within the captivation there is revelation of the creator.

Your eyelashes uncover and expose, they frame and they draw in.

Your eyes see good, they display grace.

Your eyes reveal the one who gave you breath.

His eyes, through your eyes.

One with him, one in the same, yet unique and individual because it is you.

You are beautiful; you live life beautifully.

You were born dangerous.

Believe in who you are.

God is a mystery, and so are you.

Believe in who I have called you to be.

"Yes Lord, I am yours!" she shouted.

With fresh determination Samantha came to herself, and got back up to her feet.

"I must try to get out," she said.

Directly across from her were more old tree roots growing over the wall, so she decided to climb one. She grasped the dry wood and pulled herself up, and found a place to wedge her boot into, just above the ground. She looked up at the twenty-foot wall, and with fresh resolve she began to climb hand over hand.

Some loose bark and stone came free as she reached higher. She scrunched her eyes and ducked as dirt showered down upon her. Slowly Samantha made her way up the root system and pulled herself up and onto the wall. What she saw made her heart sink. She stood upon the wall of a vast maze, dimly lit here and there by the glowing flowers. The maze that covered the landscape, and drifts of cloud and mist concealed parts of it.

Way off in the distance stood a structure; towers that looked as old and ruined as the maze itself, framed by flashes of lightning flickering in the distance. From the castle was a beam of light that rose heavenward and Samantha knew that was her way out.

Standing on the wall, surrounded by endless pathways, Samantha just stared at the castle that seemed endlessly out of reach.

"I can't go that far. I can't get all that way," she said to herself.

"No, you can't," responded the shadows.

"Be quiet!" she commanded. "I've had enough of you. Stop talking to me!" With that, a weight lifted. She then looked left and right and decided to go left. She set off running along the top of the wall. She turned right, where another wall intersected the one she was running along. Samantha kept running, making left turns and right turns, all the while getting closer to the towers in the centre of the dark lands.

Glancing up every so often to see where the castle was in relation to her, she noticed that it was drawing nearer quickly. She was covering unnatural distances.

'I'm being helped,' she thought.

Samantha slowed down as she stepped into a misty section of the maze and continued to make her way along the top of the wall. Unable to see very far in front of her, she guessed four or five turns which felt like they were leading her in the right direction. Then all of a sudden, she stepped out of the mist and found the castle towering high into the sky, directly before her.

Samantha looked back and knew that God had been helping her cover an incredible distance. 'I didn't walk that far,' she thought. 'All I had to do was start, just take the first step and keep walking, then the Lord could help me get here by his grace.'

Samantha looked for a way to climb down the wall. Walking over to a root system that covered a part of the wall like a lattice, she knelt down, and started to lower herself over. Almost immediately her boots slipped, leaving her legs dangling. She was again showered with dirt and bark. Samantha managed to maintain a firm grasp around the vines, and found a foothold to dig her toes into. After some minutes of climbing, her boots touched the brickwork that covered the castle grounds.

Samantha turned to look up at the castle again, admiring the pillar of light that blazed upwards from within it. It was the one point of hope in a darkened and ruined land. As she took a couple of steps forward towards the large arched doors, they suddenly blew off their hinges, and an enormous dragon burst out of the entrance. The dark creature roared and reared up, then slammed its front legs onto the ground.

Samantha reached for her sword but found that she had no weapons.

"How do I fight?" shouted Samantha.

"Be still," echoed the comforting strong voice that she had heard at the beginning.

Samantha stilled herself and just looked at the dragon.

The voice again spoke, "This is just your depression, and the beast is the words that you have not been healed from."

The beast continued to rear up and make noise, and pawed the ground with its claws.

"Will you forgive those who said those words? Will you let them go?"

"Lord, it's hard… but yes, I forgive… I let go."

As she said those words, the dragon lunged toward her, but Samantha remained still and stood her ground. As the beast pounced forward, it dissolved into tiny sparkles of dust, and the wind of the assault blew past her.

Then the castle in front of her started to crack and crumble. The entire structure collapsed in on itself and disappeared within the blaze of light. Samantha stepped forward and into the brightness. As she did the darkness receded. Samantha came back to herself and found that she was still trapped under the debris, still under water, having been pinned for who knows how long.

"I'm still here!" she yelled out. Oxygen was running low, and so was the opportunity to complete her mission.

Suddenly a ribbon of light wound around her arms. She immediately felt a rush of adrenaline through her body. It was the prayer that Liberty had prayed while she and Falcon were at the river deciding what to do next. She pushed up again with prayer-backed strength, and the object was thrown off. Samantha, then quickly swam out from under it before it could settle back in place again. She could see nothing but plumes of dust and sediment clouding the waters. She swam away to a safe distance and turned to see what the object was. As she did, she saw another object falling towards her. She kicked away again, retreating a safe distance. The second object landed in another cloud of dirt and dust.

They appeared to be large doors, or something of the sort.

'They're just dumping stuff. And they're dumping it on me!' Samantha thought, feeling frustrated that discarded trash had held her for so long.

She swam around the perimeter of the pile of debris. 'They don't even care about the environment! A magnificent crystal city hangs in this lake, but underneath, the demons just litter it with all their junk!'

As she swam, the glow of her medallion grew stronger. 'Hope it's not buried too far down,' she thought.

As she got halfway around the dumping ground she noticed that the brightness of her medallion started to dim. She went back to where it was the brightest, and swam forward over the debris, this time very aware of what could be dropped from above.

At what looked to be full brightness of her medallion, Samantha started to dig and pull away boxes and shelving and worn pieces of armour. A golden object caught her eye. 'Perhaps a gem or a golden ornament?' she thought. She brushed away the dirt and ran her fingers down a long smooth surface.

'That's it!' she thought excitedly. Samantha took hold of it, dislodging it from the mud. She wiped it down and held it up. 'It is the arm of the throne. I've found it!'

She strapped it to her back and swam back towards the city. With the piece of the throne in her possession, she felt a fresh determination to complete the assignment that she had been set. She felt confident that she would be able to return the armrest of the throne to its rightful place.

Once the city was in sight again, she turned off her lights. Looking around, she searched for where Trillion had said that there would be a light tunnel. She couldn't see any light tunnel immediately.

'He said it might be hard to find,' she thought. Far enough away from the city, so as not to be seen, she continued to swim around in wide arcs, hoping to see the tunnel soon.

Just then, she a faint flash of light over to her right off in the distance. 'Could be it!' she thought and swam over to get a closer look. As she drew near, she saw another two flashes of light, and became confident that she was looking at a light tunnel. Swimming up to it, she saw it extending off into the distance in opposite directions. The display on her forearm indicated that breathing time was running out - three bars. The plan was to wait until she only had two bars left to jump into the tunnel. The girls needed to synchronize their advance on the throne.

'After all that,' she thought. 'I still have some time to wait!'

Samantha found a rock beside the tunnel and sat on it, looking out through the hazy waters, and waited.

29

DUNGEONS

- mission trinity -

"Trinity, you will have Shar to cloak you as you take the submerged pathways to the dungeons," said Seraph.

Trinity looked at Shar with a smile. Shar looked back with a confidence in his eye that was comforting for her.

"But don't you leave me down there!" Trinity said playfully, pointing to him.

"If I get you in, I'll also get you out," responded Shar.

Then he added, "You do realise that even though you have been cloaked by me, I've never cloaked you before?"

"Yea, I've done this. I know, must make me superior," Trinity said, even though Shar of course was much more powerful. Trinity immediately thought, 'Oops, a case of my mouth running ahead of my brain again.'

Shar saw the humour of it and gave a small chuckle.

"Anyway," he said. "You know the drill, as long as you walk close beside me, under my robe, we will appear as one. But remember, it is your form that they will see, so don't look into their eyes or they will know that you are human. Also, I'll only be able to cloak you up to a certain point before we will need to find some place to rest, but we will work it out on the way. Let's go."

Walking as far as they could to the causeway before being noticed, Shar said, "Are you ready? We will have to move quickly."

"Yes," Trinity responded with a smile.

"Shar stood with his arm out and Trinity stepped under his cloak. Immediately the cloaking took place. Trinity immediately took the form of an angel and the two began walking out towards the lake.

Trinity stepped onto the wide glassy causeway and quickly strode towards the main entrance. The causeway was completely smooth and flat, suspended just above the surface of the water. She passed groups of angels and demons, but made no eye contact, walking straight ahead. As she got closer, she looked up at the towering wonder. The glassy structures, crafted by what could only be spiritual wisdom birthed in eternity, rose high into the sky, shining in the sunlight, and reflecting various shapes of light onto the surface of the waters.

As she passed through the main entrance, into a large and ornate atrium, Shar whispered, "Over to the left." She obeyed and navigated around groups of spirit beings. She stole glimpses of the environment around her. The architecture looked like ice carvings, with grand staircases in all directions, some leading upwards to higher levels, and some descending below the waterline. There were even huge chandeliers, unbound by the laws of physics, hanging on nothing, dispersing rays of light.

'Demons have no right to be in such a grand place like this!'

Trinity thought.

Shar whispered again, "Just over there, that second staircase, going downwards. We will take that one."

"Are you holding up okay?" asked Trinity.

"Yes, good," Shar responded. "I can hold this cloak for a while. Let's keep pushing on."

They descended the stairwell, and then another, reaching the lower regions of the city. This part of the city had a rounded style of architecture. Above the surface it was more angular with pointed spires, and vertical columns. The submerged districts were tubular with spherical rooms, interconnected by glassy tunnels. The appearance of the structural framework reminded Trinity of diagrams of molecules with spheres representing atoms, and connecting lines representing bonds.

The glass tunnels were narrow in places, just the width of three or four people across, so they would have to be careful, maintaining faith, while being in close proximity to demons.

They walked for a long time from room to room, and chamber to chamber. Trinity then stepped into a large circular room and was able to look out at the waters in every direction. Even though the water was hazy, she could see the lakebed stretching out for quite a distance. There was nothing much to look at, just some rocks with plants growing between them. No fish.

As she got about halfway across the room, she noticed a pocket of bubbles rise up against the glass. As she kept looking, another small puff of bubbles rose a bit further along. The bubbles were visible all the way up the high wall-line, then peeled off the roof and continued to rise to the surface.

'Something's down there,' she thought. Then she remembered, 'Oh, and Samantha is out there too somewhere.'

Then it suddenly dawned on her, 'What?' she thought. 'Is that Samantha?' Through the convex glass, everything outside the submerged room was magnified and so anything outside of the ordinary would be noticed.

Trinity looked up and a group of demons were about to walk into the room from a tunnel on the far side, and there was a very good chance that those bubbles would catch their attention.

"Shar!" Trinity whispered urgently. "I think that's Samantha out there. Those demons may see her."

"Get ready," he responded. "We will need to draw their attention onto us. Walk directly towards the demons, so that they will have to move out of the way. Hopefully that will be enough of a distraction."

Up ahead the demons noticed Trinity walking toward them and shuffled to the side to give her room. When they noticed that she had not changed her course, offering the same decency that they had offered her, but was walking directly toward them, they stopped what they were doing. Trinity did not look up, keeping her identity concealed.

'What do I do now?' thought Trinity. 'Keep walking?' Her next move was decided for her. The demon in front drew its sword, and said to her in a deep voice, "What do you want?"

Trinity stood still in front of them. She most definitely had their attention. Two of the other demons also drew their swords.

"Fine!" said Trinity, she looked up and stared directly at them. The demons looked at her in complete astonishment, realising that a girl stood in front of them. Trinity attacked first, reaching for her sword. As she did, Shar uncloaked and drew his sword. Suddenly the one became two, taking the demons thoroughly by surprise. Trinity slashed the closest demon, causing it to burst into a ball of flame, which then reduced into a cloud of black, sooty smoke. Shar jumped high and brought his blade down on the demon in front of him, splitting it into two, expelling more smoke. He then swept his blade across, slashing his next opponent which also disintegrated. Trinity defended a blade, then thrust hers through the next creature. Finally, with skilful handling of her sword, she finished off the remaining two demons that had opposed her. By now there were clouds of heavy smoke lingering in the air.

"Let's run before others come," said Shar. "It'll clear soon. Follow me to the dungeons."

They took off through another tunnel, then took the next on their left leading down to an even lower level. Suddenly up ahead, Shar raised his hand into a fist, indicating to stop. He threw himself against the side of the tunnel, so as not to be seen. Trinity did the same. Shar lifted his cloak and Trinity slid under it again. Up ahead was a large room and she could tell from the sound that there was a lot of activity up ahead.

She whispered to Shar, "What do you see?"

"I can't believe it," he said. "See over there on the wall. That's the piece of the throne. That's what we've been looking for. But, the room is full of enemies."

"You must be right, my medallion is glowing. What do we do?" said Trinity.

Just then a siren went off, along with some unintelligible announcement. All the demons were startled, then began to shout.

"What's that?" asked Trinity.

"It's an alarm," said Shar. "I bet it's for us, or Samantha or Layla."

Suddenly the demons all rushed as one out of the room, through a side tunnel. They all went on mass to apprehend the intruder.

"Now's our chance!" said Shar, and ran forward, into the room, and towards the piece of the throne.

30

shattered

- mission trinity -

"Oh, it's behind glass!" exclaimed Trinity, as she got to the wall. "It's in a glass box."

Feeling the pressure of the moment, and feeling impulsive Trinity raised her sword.

"No, wait!" called Shar.

But it was too late. Trinity brought her sword hard down on the glass, which shattered into thousands of pieces. As the box shattered a terrible thing happened. Immediately metal spikes from the wall thrust themselves through the arm of the throne, which bent and broke it into pieces. Parts of it were left hanging on the wall, with the spikes protruding from it, while other parts of it fell to the floor.

"No!" said Shar. "It's destroyed!"

Trinity looked at it in disbelief at all the pieces. They couldn't put it back together again. The defence mechanism had done its job."

"What now?" asked Trinity.

"There is nothing more we can do here," responded Shar. "Change of plan."

Trinity could now hear voices again. "They're coming back," she said.

Shar looked up, as if listening. Then he said, "You'll need faith for this. You may not like it."

"Just tell me!" said Trinity, who was feeling ready to fight, or do whatever it took to achieve success for their quest.

"Here," said Shar, as he held out his hand. Trinity reached out and took what was being given to her. It was a piece of cloth folded up. The white silky cloth shimmered in the light as she flipped it over and ran her fingers along its surface.

"What's this for?"

"It's for you to wear, to cover your eyes"

"A blindfold. Are you joking?!"

"Peter would have been better off with one of these walking on the water don't you think?"

"Well... yeah... I guess he wouldn't have noticed the waves as much. But this is way different. That's like taking a walk in the park compared to..." when Trinity realised what she was saying, she decided not to finish her sentence. Walking on water was pretty impressive after all. No point arguing with Shar who was obviously on a higher level of thought than she was.

"I need to leave this with you," said Shar. "I have to go. There's nothing more I can do." With that, Shar drew his hand across his body. A horizontal strip of light appeared next to him. Then the light broadened like a door being opened to a bright room on the other side. Shar spun around and stepped through the opening, being engulfed in the light. For a moment there was a strong wind that blew through the doorway as it closed up. Then it was gone.

"Great!" said Trinity. "Not a weapon, just a piece of cloth. Thanks!"

Knowing that she needed to get her faith on, Trinity put the blindfold on and tied it securely behind her head. Suddenly she heard a number of enemies burst into the room.

"Got you!"

Her whole body suddenly felt restricted as she found herself caught in the grasp of a large demon.

"Do we throw her out into the lake?" said one voice.

"No!" came a yell. "Chief wants her."

Trinity was hoisted over the demon's shoulder, held tightly with her arms pinned to her sides, unable to move.

She was taken through various passages to one of the underwater dungeons and set in front of a chief. She remained in the grasp of the large demon so that she could not take off the blindfold.

"What do we have here then? It's the girl. Ha, and I get to see you before I kill you. You have failed. You could not complete your mission. Oh, and your friend who is swimming around in the lake, we are about to dispatch our forces against her too. Neither of you are going to complete your mission. You are too weak."

"Yes I am," replied Trinity, almost involuntary. 'Why am I agreeing with this demon?' she thought.

"Yes! You said it yourself. You are totally incapable of completing your mission or saving your friend. You in fact are quite useless. You lost and now you will die!"

Trinity opened her mouth with words that she did not expect. But as she said them, she knew immediately how powerful they were… "But, it's not about me."

"What?!" said the demon. "It is entirely about you and your weakness."

"If it was, then I wouldn't have gotten this far." Then Trinity yelled out. "It is about Jesus and what he has done. He has the victory!"

With that, there was an explosion which reverberated around the room. The grasp around her dropped and she fell to the floor. The thundering eventually stopped and all was quiet. Trinity lifted the blindfold and found herself in a vast empty room with many scorch marks and countless wisps of smoke.

'There must have been hundreds of them,' she thought. Then she realised, 'Lord, you allowed me to be caught so that I could confront one of the chiefs and destroy the enemy's work in one single blow! Not only have I eliminated a large chunk of enemy forces, I've also helped to save Samantha who is still out there somewhere.'

"Even if I have lost my piece of the throne, surely there is more I can do. I must get back to the shore and see if I can find the others."

Just then a sliver of light appeared, and Shar emerged again.

"What!? You missed all the action! You went on lunch-break while I contended with an entire army!"

"You did a great job," Shar responded.

"No thanks to you!" she said jokingly.

"You took out more with a single blow than I could have ever done had we been fighting. This battle needed to be won through revelation, without your eyes being focussed on the surrounding situation."

"True! And we did it. So thank you," said Trinity.

"I can cloak you again from here. Let's go," said Shar.

They quickly stole through the tunnels. Running in one, then out of another, they rose through the many levels. They made it up the staircase and into the main foyer. There were very few demons in the foyer now. The alarm had evidently caused them to assemble elsewhere. Shar and Trinity stepped out onto the causeway, still with the faint sounds commotion behind. For now all they could do is make their escape. They ran the length of the causeway, stepped onto the shore of the lake, then ran across to their original hiding place.

Trinity began to feel remorseful again, as the memory of the fragments of glass, and destroyed piece of the throne flashed in her mind.

"I took matters into my own hands instead of waiting for you," she said.

"Yes you did," responded Shar.

"Hey! Aren't you going to tell me that it's going to be aright; that we are going to complete our mission?" asked Trinity, who was feeling the weight of her actions.

"But that wouldn't be the truth," replied Shar.

"Oh, no," sobbed Trinity, with tears welling up in her eyes. The thought of her friends faces came to mind, and how disappointed they would be. Trinity had a growing realisation of her actions effecting others, like waves rolling out, influencing the lives of those she loved. She felt broken, helpless and repentant. A gaping empty space opened up within her, waiting to be filled. That was what God needed. In response to her repentance, a single drop of love splashed into her heart. After that another drop followed.

Trinity took a deep breath and said to God, "I'm sorry." Then a flow of love washed over her and she was filled with the presence of the Holy Spirit. Shar could sense what was happening and so remained silent.

There were no more words needed. The two looked back across the lake. All was astir within the city.

31

PROJECTION

- mission LAYLA -

Layla sat on a rock, watching her friend wade into the water. Samantha turned and waved; her capable silhouette framed by the bright vertical lines of Crystal City. Layla waved back. Once she was just over waist deep, Samantha dived into the water and disappeared from sight. All that remained were circular ringlets that expanded across the surface of the lake.

Layla looked out toward the Crystal City, populated with angels and demons walking along the multiple glassy skyways, many storeys high. Her eyes ran down the smooth glassy structures, through surface of the lake, extending to the depths far below.

Seraph interrupted her thoughts, pulling her back into the moment as he spoke, "Layla, you need to retrieve the headrest that has been broken off, then get to the throne itself. Your path is the most exposed, so there is little margin for error. Fortunately we know exactly where the headrest has been taken. Let me show you."

Layla slid off the rock she had been sitting on, and came up alongside Seraph as he pointed to a particular spire and then explained the pathway she should take.

"…And beyond that, is the throne, in the centre courtyard. You will be able to see it from the spire," Seraph instructed.

"But the big problem is how you are going to get there," said Seraph. "Well, it's not a problem as such," he said, correcting himself. "But what I'm going to suggest hasn't been done before.

"We can't cloak you because it's too far and too exposed. I can't fly you in either. The enemy is continually searching the skies and there are many adversaries around the throne. So the only possibility we can see is… you will need to time-run."

"Time-run?!" exclaimed Layla. "What's that?"

"Time-running is theoretical. Angels can't do it, and we haven't seen it done. But it is possible for you to run ahead of yourself for a margin of time. The time river is fluid, and entities within the river are also fluid. So, we could pull you out in two different places, the real you out first, then we can pull out your projection afterwards. The spirit realm will be able to see your projection which could be a few minutes behind, but the real you will be invisible to the realm, until…"

"Until what?!" asked Layla with raised eyebrows.

"Until your projection catches up," replied Seraph.

"Oh, why didn't I think of that?!" she said, rolling her eyes, thinking that this mission was getting more and more extreme as time went on. But she was willing to stretch her faith, and do whatever it took to achieve her mission. So, with a smile she said, "Well then, let's go and create me a spiritual shadow!"

"Yes, you could look at it like that," responded Seraph. "You will be perhaps five minutes ahead of yourself to start with. The enemy will see your projection coming and will know that you are attempting to take the throne, so they will launch a full-scale assault. Your projection will keep running through the blades, and all the time catching up to you. Try not to get held up, because once your projection catches up, the enemy will know exactly where you are. You'll be able to see your projection coming too, and will get a sense of how much time you have to get to your piece of the throne."

"I get it," said Layla. "I just have to keep moving, outrunning my projection for as long as I can until I get to the throne."

"That is right," said Trillion. "You are setting off last because the enemy will see you coming."

***

A time river outlet flowed nearby. Layla, Trillion and Seraph got to the entrance of the river and stepped through the glassy tunnel onto the narrow bank. The tunnel was filled with the noise of rushing water.

"So Layla…" said Trillion, in a raised voice so he could be heard. "Wait for a few minutes so we can position ourselves along the bank. You will only be in the river briefly before I pull you out. Then run! Gain as much time as you can before your projection is pulled out. We can't let your projection travel too far down river, or it will become disconnected from you and will be lost. If your projection breaks away, you will no longer be held here. You'll find yourself back in Riverdale and the quest will fail. So Seraph will go down river and grab your projection before that happens. He will throw it out, then it will be all on. Demons will attack your projection and hopefully it takes them long enough to work out what is going on. You ready?"

"Yes!"

"I'll give you the signal, then jump."

Layla watched the two make their way along the narrow bank. Trillion stopped, and Seraph continued walking a ways down river. The rushing of water continued to fill her ears. Trillion raised his hand and gave the 'thumbs up'. Layla held her breath and jumped. She flapped her arms, then almost straight away, she was yanked from the water and flung into the air. Layla twisted her body around, dive-rolled onto the ground, then up to her feet, and ran.

Her boots pounded along the shoreline as she steadied her breathing, knowing that she could be on the run for up to a couple of hours. She then turned onto the main glassy causeway suspended over the water, leading into the great glistening city. Layla looked up, seeing the layers and layers of walkways, criss-crossing the sky above her, and she knew that she had a long way to go. Off in the distance, behind many buildings was the spire that Seraph had pointed out, protruding through the skyline.

Layla looked for the largest open spaces between those populating the city. At the same time she kept in mind the direction she should take. The Holy Spirit was giving her mental clarity to understand her path.

As she got deeper into Crystal City, she had to take more care so as not to bump into a demon, or an angel for that matter. As long as her projection was a good distance from her, she was relatively safe. Though, she was mindful that if she happened to run through a demon blade, it would kill her, dumping her out of the realm.

As she got closer toward the centre of the city, she traced her eyes, from building to building and walkway to walkway. She spotted a tall building with many skyways and few demons, and went for it.

As she entered the building, a handful of demons ran past her, and she thought she could hear a growing commotion outside. Layla looked back and couldn't see her projection yet, but knew it wouldn't be far behind.

Layla, bounded up many stairs at a time, and out onto a portico, high above the lake. The view was spectacular, but there was no time for sightseeing. She ran into an adjacent building and out onto another walkway. As she looked below, she saw her projection for the first time, running along a walkway lower down. It was being attacked by multiple demons who were angrily trying to slash at it and having no effect. As she looked down, her projection looked up.

"What?!" said Layla. "Don't freak me like that!" she said to herself, waving her hand through the air as if to direct her projection to look elsewhere. As she did, her projection waved her hand back with a frown, as if to say, "Mind your own business! Stop looking at me and get on with your own job!"

'Yep that's me alright!' she thought. A couple of demons looked up, but seeing nothing, continued attacking the projection. Fortunately her projection was doing a good job of avoiding blades and arrows and other weapons, keeping the game alive.

Her projection looked up again with an expression on her face as if to say, 'This isn't a holiday you know – just keep moving!'

'Well that's freaky,' thought Layla. 'I'm now fighting with my own projection and getting annoyed at myself… Is that how I look when I'm annoyed? I need to work on that.' The sudden revelation of self-awareness was a bit too confronting. Layla pushed her thoughts aside for now and continued to do her best to outrun her projection.

Suddenly, up ahead five demons burst out of the doorway, leaving no room for her to pass. With only moments before impact, Layla dropped off the walkway and spun to grip the edge with her fingers, while the rest of her body dangled high above the streets of the city. She tried to pull herself up, but then noticed more and more demons pouring onto the walkway.

Layla looked to the sky, with her grip weakening and cried out, "Help!"

32

SPIRE

- mission Layla -

Back on-surface Layla's mother, who was an artist, was working on a painting in her studio. As she swept brushstrokes over the canvas, with worship music playing, she felt the presence of the Lord. Then Layla came to mind and so she prayed, as she usually did. As she turned her thoughts heavenward, small blades of glory rose from the floor. She put down her paint brush, got up from her desk, and started to pace and pray. The blades grew like grass covering the floor of the studio. Then golden plants and flowers rose around her. The flowers opened releasing pops of fragrant energy. Within minutes, an entire garden had formed within the studio and then in a unified burst of energy, all the flowers, plants and trees released a shower of glory into the air.

Spring was in full season within the eco-chamber of the studio. Answers, possibilities and heaven's solutions were released. Then, having achieved full bloom, the seasons shifted. Spring and Summer quickly passed, and the garden receded back down into the floor again. Layla's mother returned to her chair, stretched her arms out, then picked up her paintbrush. With a smile on her face, and fresh inspiration, she continued to paint.

***

Suddenly Layla smelt a wonderful fragrance around her, like a garden full of flowers. It was the fragrance of the Holy Spirit. Suddenly she felt energised. Her muscles felt strong, and she felt like running. Her hands and fingers tensed and she started to swing her body. With one big push, she launched herself up onto the walkway and started to run again, towards the next wave of opponents that had burst out of the doors up ahead.

Still invisible to them, she rushed forward launching into the air, and dived over the first two. Back on her feet, she dodged left, then right, and around the next couple of demons. Layla then cartwheeled through a narrow gap between two hulking demons, then back flipped over the last one in the group, spun, and kept running.

She bounded up another spiral staircase, then threw herself against a wall, narrowly dodging a group, charging past her. The staircase opened out onto a wide covered colonnade with rows of arches either side, casting shadows across the landing. As she ran, she saw three demons running toward her shoulder to shoulder up ahead, leaving no room for her to manoeuvre around. The ceiling was too low to dive over them and with rows archways either side her options were limited. With little time to think, she drew her sword, and grasping it with two hands, raising it over her shoulder, she darted right, and swung her sword with all of her might, cutting through armour, flesh and bone of the two demons on her right. As they fell to pieces on the ground the third demon jumped away in fright and drew its axe. Layla spun around, and walking up to the third demon which was staring down at the other two in disbelief, Layla put an end to its surprise. Its axe clanged, as it struck the floor.

As she looked up, she saw a large demon walking toward her wearing large goggles.

"I see you!" it bellowed and rushed toward Layla. It raised an arm, then flung a rod toward Layla which spun through the air and knocked her sword out of her hand. Her sword slid along the floor, through an archway, and fell toward the lake far below.

"That was my sword!" yelled Layla angrily, who didn't feel intimidated in the slightest at this moment. She rushed at the demon, as it threw another spinning rod toward her. Layla narrowly avoided being hit by sliding under it, and then pushed herself back to her feet again. As she got close, she jumped into the air, then with all of her might, Layla kicked the demon in the side of the head which knocked it off balance as it ran. Its helmet dropped over its eyes and it ran awkwardly through an archway, dropping off the edge with a roar. The roar grew fainter as the monster fell toward the depths, hitting a walkway, and bouncing off it on the way down.

"If you want my sword, then go get it!" Layla yelled back. She continued to run into the spire at the end of the walkway, conscious that she had been losing time, and that her projection must be close.

Layla entered a room, full of relics and artifacts and charts, along with telescopes pointing out of windows. There were glass cases containing various books, weapons, jewellery, and ancient treasures.

"And yes, there you are!" she said pointing toward a beautifully crafted golden object, which could only have been the headrest of the throne. Her medallion was glowing, confirming her finding. She rushed over, unlatched the lid, and reached in. Taking hold of the piece, she drew it out.

"Stunning!" she said, admiring its craftsmanship. She then loosened some belts and secured the piece of the throne to her back, tightening the straps again, ready for the next part of her mission.

Looking out of the window facing the centre of the city, she saw the throne for the first time, situated in the middle of a courtyard below her. It was amazing to finally see the throne of Geneva, the goal of her mission, that she had fought so hard to get to. It looked grand. The ancient craftsmanship was exquisite. But it also looked broken, a shadow of what it had been.

Wondering what would be the best way to get down, she went back to the door that she had entered through, only to be met by her projection running directly toward her. It was running along the colonnade, past the arches, chased by about twenty demons.

"Nuts!"

Her projection slammed into her knocking her backwards onto the floor.

"Oh, nice to see you too!" she told herself, picking herself up, and looking at the fast approaching enemy horde.

"There must be at least twenty!" said Layla, wide-eyed.

"About forty-five," responded an angel, who had just appeared beside her.

"What?! Not helping."

"… with more on the way."

"Who are you anyway? You can't just appear like that!"

The angel reached over and closed the door to the spire and locked it. "That'll hold them back for a minute or two."

Looking the angel up and down, quickly adjusting to having a different angel helping her, she said, "So, what next?"

"We need to get you down there," the angel said, pointing out of the window.

The angel glanced around the room. Shields, armour, weapons, books.

Then he saw it, "That's it!" he said, pointing toward a golden chain draped over a chair in the corner of the room, with a shield and silver spear next to it. Layla knew what he had in mind, so rushed over and grabbed the chain and spear then went back to the window. The angel helped her quickly thread the spear through last link of the chain and threw the rest of the chain out of the window. The chain fell far below, while Layla held the spear horizontally across the window. As the chain tightened, it pulled the spear against the window frame. It lodged into the wall either side, spanning entirely across the frame.

"I'll hold them back while you rappel down. Here, use this," the angel said, pulling a flag off the wall next to him and tearing it in half. He handed her a piece at a time so that she could wrap her hands to save them from getting a friction burn. Layla then climbed onto the window frame. Just then the demons burst into the room and saw the angel with Layla silhouetted in the frame, with the light from outside shining around her.

The angel engaged, and Layla dropped from sight. She rappelled at lightning pace, down the side of the spire. Pushing out hard, she took giant leaps dropping many metres at a time. Half way down the spire, she looked up seeing the angel's head looking out of the window.

'He must be in control if he's checking on me,' she thought.

Turning her attention to the ground, she could see the enemy horde rushing around back and forth. As she got closer to the ground, with fresh determination, she saw a demon running toward her landing point. Knowing that she would connect with it, she pushed out from the wall one last time, let go of the chain and landed on the demon's head. Kicking downward with all of her might, the demon crumpled under her, breaking her fall, she rolled back onto her feet.

33

CONVERGENCE

- mission ALL -

Haans and Pierre arrived in the stagecoach just as the others had begun to pray.

"Glad you could make it," said Johan, reaching out to shake Pierre's hand. Johan had been a Christian all his life, and had always served the people of his community by making repairs to the church and helping with fencing on local farms.

"Wouldn't miss this prayer meeting!" responded Haans with a smile.

The small group of five began to pray. The little prayer meeting they had arranged didn't feel especially significant, but it was to be far more powerful than these five could ever have imagined.

As Haans prayed, his prayer-form began to emerge. Dark circles started to appear around him like burn marks or smudges on the ground. The burn marks splayed out in patterns across the grassy hill. Then within each darkened patch, a hole opened up, portals connecting one realm to another. From within each opening, Haans' prayer-form drew out small cone-shaped objects that looked like highly polished silver. Suddenly the objects were launched into the air in a patterned sequence. The prayer-rockets went up all around Haans as he prayed, with more and more being launched as he continued.

Pierre also began to pray and his prayer-form also rose. Pierre's prayer-form began as a ring of green flame around him. As he continued to press in, connecting with the Spirit of God, the flame spiralled upward. The coil of green flame burned bright and rose high above the prayer meeting.

Then an amazing thing happened. Pierre's prayer-form found a place within Haans', and Haans' within Pierre's. As the prayer-forms merged, suddenly an upwards surge blasted a hole straight through the atmosphere above them that reached the heavens.

Revolving around the pillar of power was the word 'agreement'. The word revolved around the central pillar as the group continued to pray.

Then Pierre said, "If two of us agree about anything, it will be done. We agree for favour, we agree for your kingdom to come and your will to be done!"

***

As John and William were about to walk into the council chambers together to present their papers, John said, "William, let's take a moment to pray."

"I'm with you," responded William.

As they began to pray John's prayer-form was activated again, and the gyroscopes began to spin. Having remained in an attitude of prayer all day, it didn't take long for the gyroscopes to quickly expand, rising and falling over the city. William's prayer-form combined with John's, causing it to glow and expand quicker. Other mechanics were added to it, as the gyroscopes expanded outwards across the city and the lake, and pushing out further towards Choulex. As it reached the prayer meeting, the combined prayer-forms of Haans and Pierre ignited the gyroscope with electrifying power. Surges of purple energy blazed back and forth along the arches, lighting up the sky. The entire sky was filled with blazing arches and mechanics. Shafts of light shot down to the ground, then shot back up to the sky in response to the arches revolving overhead.

***

"You didn't do it hard enough," said one demon to the next as they looked on.

"Not hard enough?!" retorted the other demon. "I knocked Pierre out didn't I?!"

"Yeah, but you could have killed him. Now he's praying and wrecking all our plans. Look, all our work is falling to pieces, our networks are tearing and breaking, and all our land is being reclaimed. Next time, trip him and throw him so he doesn't get up!"

"It wasn't just my fault. Don't forget I was just the guarantee. The infirmity spirit should have filled his lungs so he couldn't breathe. But instead, that cheeky young boy discovered the power of prayer too. We can never win!" The anxious demon looked like it was going to cry. "We've lost again. No matter what we do, God's plan always prevails. He works everything together for his purposes. It's written, you know."

"Be quiet! Don't remind me!" retorted the other spirit.

The demons continued to watch from a distance. They hated to lose, but couldn't help wanting to see what would happen next.

***

Looking down at her display, Samantha watched as three bars dropped to two.

'That's it!' she thought. 'Enough waiting around. Time to go.' Samantha swam over to the light tunnel. She braced herself, knowing that she would have to think quickly.

She took one final breath, then pulled off her helmet, and swam into the tunnel, immediately she shot through the lake and then was launched upward toward the surface. As she burst out of the waters, a dazzling sight met her eyes. The entire atmosphere was bathed in an electric purple light. The skies were all in motion with bright metallic arcs reaching across the city. Everything had movement. Skyward mechanics spun, interlocking with each other, and shafts of light rained down on the lake below.

Suddenly Samantha saw the tunnel branch off into three ahead of her. She pulled left and shot downwards with blinding speed. Heading straight towards Crystal City. Suddenly Samantha was in the courtyard, with the throne in the centre. Momentarily the tunnel flattened out along the ground giving her a split second to exit safely. With only a moment before disappearing below the ground, she rolled out.

Samantha skidded quickly along the brickwork of the courtyard grounds. With a boot in the air, she kicked a demon out of the way, and then another and another. Still at a high speed, she slammed into the wall with her boots, then pushed up onto her feet, hitting the wall with her shoulder. She bounced off the wall and spun around, ready to fight.

***

Trinity and Shar looked on at the dazzling spectacle, without their piece of the throne.

Just then a young boy walked out to the water's edge and started to look around.

Trinity noticed the boy, then pointing at him exclaimed, "What's he holding?!"

Shar looked and said, "What on earth?"

The two of them got up and raced toward the boy. He turned to face them and said, "Hello, is this for you?"

"Where did you get that? And how can you see us?" asked Trinity, very much surprised.

"Why do people keep asking me that?!" Alex exclaimed, then filled them in on his interactions with the other members of their team.

"Well, it seems that you have met just about all of us," said Trinity with a smile. She turned towards Shar holding the branch that had grown into the shape of the arm of the throne.

"Will this work? It's wood, rather than gold."

"This isn't just normal wood," Shar responded, inspecting it. "This has other properties."

"This is our piece!" he concluded.

"Great! So the next question is, how are we going to get this to the throne?"

"We will take one of those," Shar said, pointing to the sky.

The arcs continued to glide across the sky, while shooting sheets of downward light. As the light hit the ground, it shot back up to the arcs again.

"We are going to ride that prayer-form over the city," he said. "Then we will drop into the courtyard and make our way to the throne."

"Excellent! Let's make this happen!" said Trinity, with fresh confidence and excitement that she could get back into the action.

Trinity strapped the arm onto her back.

"You okay?" asked Shar. "Is the strap sturdy enough to hold it?"

"Yeah, it should be fine," she said, making a couple more adjustments. "Let's get ready to move. You set?" she asked Shar.

"Yes," he responded. "Let's move out."

The two of them ran along the water's edge watching the arcs, and taking note of when the sheets of light hit the ground to get their timing right. Bright sheets of light flashed back and forth over the city and over the waters. A sheet flashed a hundred metres in front of them, too far for them to catch. Then another sheet flashed much closer in front of them than the previous had.

Shar called, "Three more. Let's reach for the third."

A flash. "That's one," called Trinity.

Another flash, "Two," she said.

"Here we go," called Shar. "Reach!"

The two of them raised an arm and reached into the sky. Suddenly a flash fell over them. Trinity grasped the light with her raised hand and was launched into the sky. The two of them were boosted high above the lake. Trinity gasped and her eyes widened in a moment of realisation of how high she was. The world looked so small below her. She looked ahead towards the city, and fresh faith filled her heart.

"You ready for the drop?" called Shar.

"Yes!" Trinity called back, more determined than ever. 'I'm not failing this time,' she said to herself.

High over the Crystal City, Trinity saw the courtyard and throne ahead of her.

"Any second now!" called Shar, and the two of them were suddenly propelled downwards and dropped into the courtyard. They both broke their fall with a roll, and then rolled to their feet.

***

At exactly the same time, the boots of three warrior princesses hit the ground of the courtyard, and a surge of power splayed out around them.

Layla, having repelled off the spire, dropped on top of a demon, knocking it out cold. Then she rolled on to her feet and in one movement jumped into a spin kick, knocking the head of a demon into the wall beside her. She picked up the demon sword and faced the throne.

Samantha, at another end of the courtyard, had kicked a clear path for herself, bounced off the wall, and spun around picking up a sword in each hand from the demons she had knocked out.

Trinity and Shar dropped in on another side of the courtyard, powering into the enemy with hand-to-hand combat, relieving them of their weapons. They armed themselves, ready to fight their way to the throne.

Their presence could be felt by the enemy, and a sudden dread fell across all of them.

The ruined throne in the middle of the courtyard was now surrounded on three sides by the pieces that would bring it back to life and make it complete again.

The girls looked at each other with confidence. Three seasoned shieldmaidens, with one mission. 'A cord of three strands is not easily broken.' Had the enemy known who these girls were, and the faith they possessed, they would have run for their lives. Instead, with a lack of awareness and minds full of pride, with hearts full of deceit, they turned towards the girls in an attempt to defend the throne.

34

ALIGNMENT

- mission ALL -

Layla rushed forward. She lunged toward the demon in front of her, kicking it in the chest, sending it reeling backwards. She then plunged the sword into the demon behind it, dived over the top, and reaching for its axe with both hands, she ripped it out of its grasp. Swinging it through the air, she sliced through the next demon that was in her way. She threw the axe at her next opponent and knocked it to the ground. Then with power and grace, she stepped onto the fading body of the demon lying in front of her and launched into the sky. The Spirit carried her through the air, an unnatural distance, and she landed at the base of the throne. Unstrapping the backrest of the throne, and holding it in her hand, she rushed up the steps.

***

Without another thought, Samantha immediately ran forward with two demon blades held in skilful hands. She ran a blade through a demon in front of her, then swung her other blade to the side, eliminating another enemy. Spinning, with arms and blades stretched out, she cleared more space for herself, as the enemy rushed toward her. Remaining focussed and in full control, she waited a moment for more demons to come into range. Then she slid forward onto one knee, and swept her blades out left and right. The demons within the vicinity of her blades were slashed in half. She rose to her feet. As she ran forward, her faith ignited the swords. She spun them in her hands and arcs of light splayed out, giving her a greater reach. The arcs sliced through her enemies, two or three at a time. Samantha drew her arm back, then flung the sword from her right hand. It spun, flattening her enemies before her.

There remained just one large beast between her and the throne. Samantha threw her other sword which hit its mark, and stuck firmly into the beast, which stood for a moment, then fell forward. She ran over the beast that had slumped to the ground, and jumped off its back and landing on the lowest step. Unstrapping the arm of the throne, holding it firmly in her grasp as she darted up the steps.

***

Trinity and Shar were dropped within a group of demons. Trinity knocked one backward with her heel before she landed. Dangerously ready, they both drove their swords into their first opponents before even touching the ground. Then, back to back, they fought off the beasts that surrounded them. With the sound of metal on metal, they defended blades, and struck shields, slashed helmets and penetrated armour. Trinity looked up to see an arrow flying directly toward her. In an instant she raised her sword, splitting the arrow in two. She then swung her sword against the demon in front of her, kicked it backward, and finished it off. She quickly picked up the enemy shield that was lying on the ground and lifted it above her head in time to defend another two arrows. Shar came around in front of her, and with a highly skilled attack, cleared a path for Trinity so that she could make her way toward the throne. She lowered the shield to her right side to defend a blow from a spiked club. She then pushed back, releasing the shield at the same time, knocking the demon backward. The pair of them, now side by side, defended axes, swords and spears. All the time they were gaining ground, getting closer and closer to the throne. Then in a last push, Shar kicked down the demon in front of them, plunged his sword into another. Shar crouched so that Trinity could run and jump off his back. She stepped up, and pushed off, jumping over a final detachment of enemies and landed in front of the throne. Immediately she ran up the stairs with the arm of the throne in her hand.

***

The three warriors converged on the throne at the same time, and slammed their pieces into place. Each piece held fast to the throne and melded itself into a single structure. Then nothing...

"What?!" yelled Layla angrily. "Come on, what next?"

The girls turned to defend their position.

Then a booming voice shook the courtyard that caused the enemy to hold back, "You think that just bringing the pieces will restore the throne? Ha, you are sadly mistaken!"

A large kingly demon emerged from the chaos, draped in a robe, holding a sceptre.

"Before we broke the throne up, we took its power as well. See, empty!" it said pointing its sceptre at the top of the backrest. The curved piece that Layla had placed, had a hollowed out portion at the bottom of it. As she placed it together with the backrest of the throne, it created a completely hollowed out oval. Having had the hollow pointed out, it was obvious that something was missing from it.

There was a moment of silence as the three girls faced the enemies all around them. They were surrounded with nowhere to go. Then Trinity had a thought come to mind, '...hidden things to light.'

"The diamond! Where's the diamond?!" Trinity thrust her hand into her pouch, feeling around frantically. "It's not there!" she exclaimed. Then she remembered the difficulty she had in strapping the throne to herself while she was on the shore of the lake. 'Maybe it fell out then?' she thought.

***

Liberty appeared on the edge of the lake. She looked up at the brilliant gyroscopes gliding across the sky. The spectacle was incredible. Then she noticed a small figure kneeling down at the edge of the lake.

'Hello. Who's this?' she thought as she walked over. 'Oh, Alexander. That's the boy that I spoke with at the start of our mission. What's he doing? Is he praying? And what's that in his hand?'

As Liberty came up beside him, she heard him muttering under his breath, praying to Jesus.

"He will help save this city," the Holy Spirit said to Liberty.

"Really?! You mean he's met you now? He's become a Christian?"

"Yes."

"Wow! I was about to pass him by, to get on with my mission and follow John. I'm so glad that I took the time to encourage him to go to church," Liberty responded.

"Yes, Liberty, you made a wise choice. Famous people may be the ones who seem to shape the world, but the prayers of this young boy, with childlike faith, has a big part to play in shaping the direction of this city."

Liberty looked on in wonder at the boy. The thing in his hand started to glow. Then he threw it and it shot from his hand high into the sky and toward Crystal City. The boy looked up with a smile as he tracked the diamond with his eyes soaring like a shooting comet.

***

A bright object caught Trinity's attention. She looked up just in time to see a shooting star hurtling toward her. Instinctively she knew it was the diamond. She jumped high to reach it and caught it in her hand.

The king demon roared out, "No!"

Knowing what to do next, Trinity stepped over to the throne and placed the diamond within the oval. Immediately the throne blazed, and in a pulse of energy thrust the girls backwards. The entire courtyard was flattened and all the demons were swept outwards and crushed against the walls of the courtyard. The girls and the angel, even though knocked off their feet by the blast, were not thrust against the wall. They felt the strong surge, but the effect was far more pronounced on the enemy who were being cleared out of the courtyard, crushed against the walls and squeezed out of the realm. They disappeared a few at a time, roaring and yelling as they were displaced.

The throne looked like liquid metal as the pieces all became one.

Suddenly a bright blue tube of light shot up from around the throne and blazed into the sky. As the blue light touched the purple arcs rising and falling over the city, it absorbed all the blue colouring of the purple arcs so that the arcs became red. Then from the central blue pillar, a sheet of blue light shot out either side. A wall of light shot northward, and another wall stretched out southward. The first triaxial identifier was set up.

***

As the five continued to pray, with Tristan, Caden and Jack standing behind them, making sure that there would be no disruption to this prayer meeting, a faint glow started to develop between them. As they continued to call on the name of the Lord Jesus Christ, the glow grew into a mist. The mist rose rise high into the sky and as it touched the arcs, all the red pigment that had saturated the arcs was drawn towards the mist. As the red colour was drawn out of the atmospheric mechanics, the arcs became golden. Then all the red colour shot downwards into the middle of the prayer warriors and suddenly there was a great flash of red light. Tristan, Caden and Jack were all thrown backwards. When they were able to open their eyes again and look up, there before them, was the Elemental Stone spinning in all its brilliance, suspended above the ground in the middle of the group of prayer warriors. Then, as they looked on, a fan of light pushed outwards and upwards, extending West and East.

"The triaxial identifier!" shouted Caden. "It's been set up!"

Jack smiled, knowing that they had achieved what they had set out to do. A wall of red hung in the sky before them. As the three looked West, from their position at Choulex, toward the city they could also see the blue triaxial identifier, intersecting the red one. Two walls of light hung clearly in the air confirming that the throne and the atmosphere had been won.

"We've done it!" said Tristan with a big smile. "The red and the blue are in alignment. I hope Liberty has got to the altar."

35

ALTAR

- mission Liberty -

As Liberty looked from the shoreline at the two triaxial identifiers hanging in the air, slivers of light appeared either side of where she was standing. There were two rows, about five shafts of light on each side. As they opened up, angels started to appear, many angels. As Liberty stood her ground, she found herself surrounded by about fifty angels.

"Uh, hello," she said. "Why are you all here?"

One angel stepped forward and said, "We are here for the final battle. The red and blue triaxial identifiers have been set up. We know the enemy has the keys to the altar. So we must take our final stand around the altar to defend it, and we need you."

"You may not have to defend it," responded Liberty. "The keys have been swapped, or rather the slots in the altar have. So when the enemy inserts them into the wrong slots, it will actually be the correct ones!"

"I don't know what you've done, or how you've done it," said the angel, "but we must go to make sure that what needs to be done, must get done. Please come with us."

Liberty nodded her head. The angels then retreated through the openings of light and Liberty followed. The lights closed and they were gone.

***

Liberty stepped into the place in-between, following the squadron of angels. She found herself surrounded by liquid light; the fiery hem of eternity. She looked at the angels who were all distorted by the extreme brightness. It was like being in the midst of golden raging fire.

A hand rested on her shoulder, "This way," the angel said, then walked ahead indicating the way she should go. As she followed, she could hardly see where she was going. Within the blaze of the in-between realm, all she could see was distorted figures here and there in front of her. They came to a huge fiery wall. A narrow pathway opened up before them and the angels in front of her stepped through.

She felt tiny, as she followed the narrow pathway between the towering, raging walls either side. She wondered how the angels could navigate through such a blaze when all around her looked and sounded like a ferocious furnace.

Suddenly the angel in front disappeared. Liberty took another step and was herself swiftly pulled. She felt the front of her being taken hold of, like being jerked forward by a giant magnet. Liberty was stretched between two points. Then the back half of her body caught up, and she could see all the angels again. She was still within the blaze, but in a different part of the realm. 'Is this how they travel?'

she thought.

Then she heard a shout from the front, "They're here! They knew we were coming!"

Suddenly all around her was movement. Silhouettes of what looked like angels and demons were engaged in combat. Some were fighting on the plane that she was standing on. Some looked like they were fighting on other planes of existence within the inferno, some on horizontal planes, some on vertical planes, and some on other angles. They looked to be in other places within the realm, but she could still see them through the distorted golden energy.

"Get her out!" she heard an angel shout. Then she was picked up by both shoulders, and flown through the blaze. They soared between the raging elements. Liberty looked up at her escort and felt comforted that she was in the hands of a mighty angel.

'I want to help,' Liberty thought. So she prayed, 'Lord, give your servants victory today…'

Liberty saw that they were approaching another fiery wall.

"One more transition," said the angel. Instead of the wall opening up this time, the angel swooped and pulled up, throwing Liberty, so that her boots landed on it. As the angel let go, reality tilted and she found that she could stand.

"Walk forward," the angel shouted, "through the pyramid. I'll hold off the enemy."

Liberty turned to see the shape of the angel disappear through the blaze. Once again alone, all she could do was follow instructions. She walked forward. Deciding walking was too slow, she picked up the pace and broke into a run. As she did she noticed her surroundings closing in, and the blaze becoming more intense. She realised that above her were two more planes either side, leaning against each other to create a triangular gap. As she ran forward, the triangular tunnel became smaller until she could reach out either side to touch the walls. They were liquid and solid at the same time. Solid to push against, but moving at the same time, like shallow, fast flowing rivers.

One more step, and the same magnetic pull propelled her forward. She was drawn out of the place in between and stepped into the chamber of the altar. The blaze behind her narrowed and closed, and there before her was the altar with the enemy hordes surrounding it.

Crouching down behind a rock, she knew that she hadn't been noticed yet. From her vantage point she could see five large demons standing elevated above the crowd, around the altar. The familiar altar was just as she had seen it when it was being created. The only differences was that the keys were not circling above it, and the altar was surrounded by the enemy.

Then a booming voice said, "The humans have set up the atmosphere, and they have also set up the throne, but we have the altar!" There was a cheer and a roar from the horde.

"Now, we could insert the keys for ourselves, and undo all of their work, and plunge this city into darkness, but we have decided to wait."

'What?!' thought Liberty. 'No, you can't wait. You must insert the keys, so that we can finish our mission!'

"Yes, we will wait!" said the demon again. "Our new strategy is to wear the Christians out! To play the long game! They feel so close, but they won't get their breakthrough, and so they will have to wait. We could hit them with the altar, but then in the midst of adversity, in the midst of persecution, they may eventually rise up. We will go for the less obvious approach, and cause them to drift away and lose their passion."

"Yes!" shouted the demons. "Lose their passion!"

'No!' thought Liberty. 'I must get those keys back, but where are they?' It was then that she noticed on the far side of the chamber, hanging on the wall, what looked like the keys.

"So these will stay with us!" shouted the demon who turned to point at the keys on the wall.

"Yes, that's them," said Liberty under her breath.

"We will take the keys, and bury them deep in the heart of our kingdom, far away from any hope of discovery."

Liberty looked for a way around the chamber. There were rocks around the edge, like the one she was hiding behind, but it was unlikely that she would be able to get all the way around without being noticed.

Then she thought, 'Light tunnels. Are there any of those here?'

Her eyes searched for any kind of faint glow, and one caught her attention.

'Yes, there's one. Oh, and there's another.'

The two tunnels criss-crossed each other, one just above her at head height, and the other high up at the top of the chamber. Both tunnels arced. The lower tunnel entered the chamber through the wall over to her left, and curved around to exit the chamber very near where the keys were. Unfortunately, to jump into that tunnel would require her running over to it, covering too much ground, and she would surely be stopped before she got there. The other light tunnel had quite a different path, it curved up and over the top of the chamber. As she tracked it back with her eyes from the top of the chamber, she saw that at ground level it was quite close to where she was.

'Perhaps I could make it to the vertical tunnel, then drop into the other curved tunnel below, and drop out again next to the keys. Maybe I could swipe the keys, then get back into the tunnel again?'

The demons looked like they were about to move, then they would take the keys, and they would be gone forever. Now was the moment. Liberty made a dash. Halfway to the tunnel a demon turned and spotted her and let out a roar. As it charged, Liberty drew her sword and slashed her enemy in two. She caused a commotion, but it didn't matter. Two more steps, and she leapt into the tunnel. Knowing it would be fast, she risked turning out of it almost instantly and fell through the air. She stretched out her body, reaching for the other tunnel, and she managed to catch it with her arms. The tunnel drew her whole body into it, and she shot again around the chamber. Turning again, almost instantly, she dropped out of the tunnel near the keys. But then a big whack knocked her backwards and into the wall. One of the demons near the keys reached up and snatched them off the wall.

"Over here!" bellowed one of the five demons near the altar. The keys were thrown, then caught near the altar.

"You humans never give up!" it shouted angrily. Then it said, "It is time to finish you off. Forget the plan. How do you like this?!" With that, it took a key in each hand and walked over to the altar. Frustrated that it was going for Plan B, but at the same time feeling victorious, it looked at the slots, making sure that it had the opposite key in each hand. It then raised its arms and slammed the keys into the slots on the altar.

There was an explosion, and then a suspension. The explosion had knocked a number of demons in the vicinity off their feet, then they were held in mid-air. The altar had created its own gravity-time field and all was suspended around it within a blue glow. Liberty was also floating, but she found that she could move, able to swim through the gravity field. Evidently the demons couldn't.

'Did it work?' she thought.

She pushed herself through the air and drifted between demons who were caught in an empty timelessness. Liberty reached the altar and placing both hands on it, she pulled her legs down to a standing position.

She studied the slots and the keys, then whispered, "Yes!"

The top of the altar opened up into a spherical time-portal enabling her to see what was to come. She looked in wonder. The world moved on, dispensations opened and closed, constellations shifted. Vast tracts of time rolled over like wind-swept leaves turning over a courtyard. Geneva shone and became great.

"It worked," she said. With that the explosion came to life again, and blew outwards, blasting all the demons within the chamber to the outer edges. Liberty remained in the centre. The altar began to glow and then a golden shaft of light shot upwards. The triaxial identifier was raised high into the sky and expanded into a wide blazing pillar that blasted through the roof of the chamber and lit up the atmosphere.

***

Just as the words came out of Tristan's mouth, "I hope Liberty has got to the altar," a needle of golden light was raised into the sky.

"Look!" said Caden as he pointed towards it. The needle expanded to become a pillar and then opened up at the top like a giant golden umbrella. The sky was filled with the gold. Under the golden dome, the red, and the blue glowing triaxial identifiers shone.

Caden, Tristan, and Jack admired the spectacle from Choulex.

Samantha, Trinity, and Layla raised their eyes to the sky to see the three axes filling the sky with light.

"Yes! We did it," said Samantha, as she hugged Layla who was standing beside her. The three with big smiles gazed up at the walls of colour.

36

ACCEPTANCE

John Calvin walked through the doorway into the chamber with his documents neatly arranged under his arm. Feeling confident and full of faith, he entered with a large smile on his face. Right behind him, William Farel also boldly walked into the room. William had a more stern look on his face, ready to lay down his arguments and refute his opponents.

John looked around the large room. The entire Grand Council was present, along with members of the public, and others, who were great supporters of John's work for the church. All were curious about what he would present. What John had not realised is that word had spread around the town that he was presenting his proposal. So when he had arrived, more people started to follow him in.

As he walked through the crowd towards his seat, his mind drifted back to 21 May 1536, when he had preached a word that swayed the Grand Council of Geneva to adopt the protestant religion. Now almost six months later, 16 January 1537, he was here to present his final articles on the Organization of the Church and its Worship at Geneva.

William had done much work during those six months, drafting and refining the confession of faith. John had also been busy writing separate articles on reorganizing the church in Geneva. Today was the day, and this was the moment.

As John looked out over a sea of grey and black council attire, he thought, 'They're hardly dressed for such an occasion. This is the Good News! This is salvation through faith in Jesus Christ! There isn't anything more wonderful than this.' Yet, as he looked out over the members of the council, they were not showing the slightest emotion.

John took his place and began to read. There was a hush as John got to the end of his first sheet of paper, picked it up, turned it over and placed it to the side. John continued to read without raising his head, not wanting to look at the stoic faces. The silence around him was almost deafening.

A thought came to mind, 'They're not going to go for this. They're already making up arguments in their head. 'What you are talking about is outlandish!' they would say.'

But at this point John decided not to listen to negative thoughts. He had done so much work that he did not care what they thought any more. He was reading the very words that God had given him and he understood the battle within the mind. He pressed on and finished the second page and looked up. The first gaze to meet his eyes was his prime adversary, the one who had already told him to his face that his preaching was 'over the top, unsettling, and even vulgar.' But more than that, John saw a demonic vulture perched on his shoulder. Chandolf was of course unaware that he was constantly being whispered to by a demonic influence. As Chandolf was about to rise to make his first defence, the entire room erupted in applause. John simply looked out at the crowd who then rose to their feet. Even if Chandolf had managed to start speaking, his voice would have been drowned out, by both the noise and the presence of God in the room. There was continued clapping and cheering as if the people had finally been given permission to praise the Lord, free to live at a higher level of life, able to express their faith in a way that connected with their soul.

The drought was over. The hunger for the Word of God had been building, looking for some kind of breakthrough to feed the hungry hearts. This was the moment, now or never to raise voices of agreement, and voices of praise to the Lord.

John could not hold back the tear that trickled down his cheek. "Father," he prayed under his breath. "Look at your people. Have mercy on them. They have found you. May they never be led astray." The love of God filled his heart and he knew that he would be their shepherd.

The presence of God fell more strongly in the room as the clapping and celebrating continued. People started laughing, some joined together and started singing. Church was never going to be the same again.

There was no need for a vote, the people had spoken and the council accepted the document on the same day. John Calvin became the spiritual leader of the city, a position created by the Grand Council as the city turned Protestant. Geneva became a centre of Protestant activity that influenced the globe from that moment onward.

37

END

Liberty was lifted off her feet. She rose within the pillar of blazing light. Quickly elevated, she looked down at the city below her through the golden lens of the Altar Axis. She could see the streets criss-crossing below her. She noticed toward the centre of the city, a large group of people were flowing out of a building. There seemed to be a lot of chatter and laughter. The Lord gave her insight into what they had been fighting for. She was looking at the City Council building, and John had just presented his piece which had been celebrated and accepted.

Most were unaware of the spiritual battle that had waged around them. All apart from one young boy that she could just make out on the ground. He was waving to her. Liberty waved back.

Caden and Tristan also rose into the air.

Jack called out from the ground, "See you in about 500 years!"

Caden and Tristan were raised higher and higher. They looked down on the small group who were still praying. Haans and Pierre had their hands raised.

"I wonder if they can sense the breakthrough," called out Caden to Tristan.

They could just make out the sound of clapping and singing and celebrating far below.

"I reckon so," Tristan responded.

The boys looked toward the city and could clearly see the red and blue axes intersecting the golden pillar. The city looked complete.

'It's in good hands now,' thought Tristan.

Layla, Samantha, and Trinity suddenly felt weightless and were drawn skyward. The brilliant shining throne looked out of place, situated in the middle of the battle-scarred courtyard. Scorch marks and gouges in the ground radiated out from the throne. It could have been a beautiful pattern had the marks not been created by demons being thrown from the blast sight. Then, as they looked, the courtyard started to transform. New paving stones appeared, following the blast lines. The entire courtyard was being repaved, preserving the lines of battle locked in beautiful brickwork. Only those who had been there at the time would know the significance of the patterns.

New life then flooded into the courtyard. Trees and plants grew around the edges and it turned into a garden in the middle of Crystal City.

The six sailed high into the sky and were able to see the bright blue and red axes extending well beyond Geneva, and beyond Switzerland.

As they were taken off into space, Liberty stretched out her arms and breathed in deeply, overjoyed having completed their quest. She thought back to the demon telling her that she had lost, that she had failed her mission. Back then it seemed that there was no way that

Geneva could ever be saved. She remembered how she felt at a loss while her and Falcon were working out their next move. But then she got the idea of going back in time. That glimmer of hope started to formulate, and it turned into a journey beyond anything she could have ever imagined.

Samantha, who was beside her, was also caught up in the sweetness of the moment. She recalled being pinned under the large doors at the bottom of the lake, unable to move with oxygen running out. She breathed deeply, thanking the Lord for the freedom to actually breathe. She also remembered overcoming her depression and those hurtful words she received when she was a child. She had stood her ground against the dragon and saw it dissolve into stardust. Samantha chuckled to herself, acknowledging that she had received some inner healing at the bottom of Lake Geneva - of all places!

Trinity loved star-gazing. Normally she would by lying on her back looking up at the sparkling canopy, but now the stars were all around her. She was in a place that was wide open and free. 'Such a contrast,' she thought, 'from being in a cave system, and running for our lives as it was collapsing around us.' She recalled the dungeons of Crystal City, and the shock of seeing the arm of the throne being torn to pieces as it hung on the wall. 'What an adventure,' she thought. 'From shock and defeat, to now being here, flying through the stars, having completed our quest!'

Gliding through space, reminded Layla of falling off the edge of the pavilion and looking up at it, quickly getting smaller as she fell. Back then, she knew nothing of where their adventures would take her, and now she could look back and see the hand of God leading all of them. She laughed to herself, remembering looking down at her own athletic projection, and the two of them getting annoyed with each other. 'But then I managed to pull myself together, as I knocked myself off my own feet! That's a first!' she thought smiling again.

Tristan looked back at the circle of the earth getting smaller and smaller and remembered falling through the floorboards, and looking up at the circular opening that got smaller and smaller as he plummeted into the depths of the earth. But now he was in a vastly different situation, gliding through the wide expanse of space, rather than being caught within the cramped confines of an electrified net. But then the spark appeared, like one of the stars that surrounded him right now. It had exploded, allowing him to escape and complete the rest of his mission. 'Thank you Lord, for help along the way!' he thought.

As they accelerated through space, Caden remembered the slow progress they had made as they climbed the pillar. He had spent hours on the rockface, but now soaring through the galaxy at an unimaginable speed. 'Some slow moments,' he thought, 'but then crazy ones too, like hitching a ride with those demon vultures! Luckily we had those leaves with us.' Caden recalled the stages of his journey, from the time river, to running through the desert, to the stagecoach, and hanging by the claws of the vulture. Those were the most memorable.

The six then landed on a flat plane which stretched out forever in front of them, like a sea of glassy gold.

An angel appeared before them.

"Congratulations," he said. "You have together achieved a great victory for the advancement of the kingdom of heaven on the earth. Heaven applauds you."

"Oh, can we go to heaven?" Trinity blurted out.

The angel smiled and said, "Let me tell you about heaven. Heaven is not a place, but a person. How can heaven be a place when it can never be pinpointed or contained? It is always expanding, never still, always moving and increasing.

"As you stand in the presence of heaven, the glory expands beneath you. It is always moving and enlarging in every direction. You are carried along within heaven as it infinitely stretches, but never gets thin. Indeed, it gets richer and deeper, thicker with glory, and more saturated with life the longer you spend there. There is only one movement and that is forward. Wherever you look is forward, wherever you move is advancement.

"Heaven is not a paradise, heaven is not a destination, and heaven is not the goal. Jesus is paradise, Jesus is our destination, and Jesus is our goal. Jesus is eternally creating and exhibiting more glory. To be with him is not where we end up, but who we journey with. Being with him, we reach further, go higher, and journey deeper. We become lost and found within his splendour, far closer to the centre than ever before."

The six stood there speechless. Then Trinity eventually said, "Oh… right."

Samantha nudged her, "Is that all you can say?! See what you get for asking a simple question?"

Then Caden added, "Whatever we are thinking, just times it by a billion, and we may start to understand the heavenly realms."

"It is good to ask questions," responded the angel, "but I have brought you here for a reason, to give you this."

The angel handed Liberty a scroll with writing on both sides.

"What is this?" inquired Liberty

"It is God's plan for the next ten years," responded the angel.

"Of this city?" asked Liberty.

"Of the world," said the angel.

"What, like the whole world? Why are you giving it to us?" Liberty asked.

"The Lord is pleased to share with his children what is to come. This applies to your time, your present, and addresses the days that you are about to step into," said the angel.

Liberty began to read aloud:

"Even as the world steps into chaos, the turmoil is confined just to the surface. The world will be blown by strong winds. Like a large tree, the leaves will be tossed about, but the thick branches, the trunk, and the roots will remain unmovable. My people will see through the chaos and will not be shaken by it. My people will be at ease because of the one in whom they trust. They will be bold, have purpose, be filled with anointing, and will be without fear. There will be earthquakes, volcanic eruptions, tsunamis, extreme temperatures, and all kinds of unrest as creation groans for what is about to come. There will be changes in leadership and in nations overnight. But my people will be unphased, trusting in me, trusting in my character.

"My people will carry Psalm 16:8 in their hearts. They will live in miracles, they will do exceptional things and not rely on the resources of the world or in the security that society offers. My people will not fear the end, and that will be a witness to the world. During this time you will find purpose and fulfilment like you have never known, and you will welcome many into the kingdom of God. Go your way, listen to the Holy Spirit, allow him to guide you and empower you with his love, and be my witness to a world that needs me."

As Liberty finished reading the scroll and looked up, she saw all around fading away and the sound of a rushing become louder and louder in her ears. Within a moment she realised she was back in the time river, being tossed about under the water. Liberty pushed up and broke the surface with a gasp. She looked around for her friends and caught glimpses of them in the river. They sailed through time once more.

Liberty got herself in a comfortable floating position and allowed the river to take her. Then after a while the sound changed and up ahead looked different. Her vision was becoming shorter, or rather, the river was running out.

'Are we getting back to the present?' she thought. Suddenly she was pushed off the edge of a waterfall with the full force of the river behind her. She fell in the midst of a shower of tonnes of water. Below was misty. She braced herself for impact, but needn't have bothered. The landing was soft as she was washed out into her lounge room. Liberty lowered her arms as she stood with the lounge materialising around her. The six found themselves facing each other, back in regular dry clothes. They all looked at each other with big smiles. The armour and the weapons had gone, but the memories and experiences would always be with them.

Then the chatter and the laughing began. The six recounted their adventures to one another until the small hours of the morning. None of them wanted to sleep. They all wanted the night to last forever. But eventually sleep caught up with them. Liberty brought in a bunch of pillows and blankets and they all drifted off one by one.

Their quest was complete, but the war was not over. What had been achieved was remarkable, but greater days were ahead. The beginning of many surface quests were about to open up.

PRAYING THROUGH
THE FRAMEWORK OF YOUR CITY

The Throne:

Pray for those in power, your leaders, those with influence.

The Atmosphere:

Speak blessing, favour, abundance, His Kingdom come.

The Altar:

Call out purpose, identity, calling, and reason for being.